I0747768

A Love Worth Waiting For

K. Lap

A Love Worth Waiting For

Copyright © 2022 by K. Lap

All rights reserved. Except for use in the case of brief quotations embodied in critical articles and reviews, the reproduction or utilization of this work in whole or part in any form by any electronic, digital, mechanical, or other means, known or hereafter invented, including xerography, photocopying, scanning, recording, or any information storage or retrieval system, is forbidden without prior written permission of the author and publisher.

Unless otherwise indicated, scripture quotations are from The Holy Bible, King James Version. All rights reserved. The Holy Bible, New International Version® NIV® Copyright© 1973, 1978,1984, 2011 by Biblica, Inc Used by permission. All rights reserved worldwide. Scriptures marked NKJV are taken from the New King James Version, Copyright ©1982 by Thomas Nelson. All rights reserved.

The scanning, uploading, and distribution of this book via internet or via any other means without the permission of the publisher and author are illegal and punishable by law. Purchase only authorized versions of this book and do not participate in or encourage electronic piracy of copyrighted materials.

This book is a work of fiction. The characters, locales, incidents, or persons portrayed in are fictitious. Any similarity to real persons, living or dead, is purely coincidental and not intended by the author. This is a product of the author's imagination.

For ordering, booking, permission, or questions, contact the author, please visit www.authorklap.com or email at keycitypro@gmail.com

Publisher: KeyCity Publishing

Cover Design: It Takes Faith Media Productions

ISBN 978-1-7364314-2-9

This book is dedicated to those who lie in wait to hold their very own baby in their arms. Though your nest may be empty now, you still long to see what God says…it may not be empty for long. Open your heart for what He has for you.

Table of Contents

Preface

I am the great I AM. I realize it is awkward having Me to write the preface, but indeed, it is Me. I am the Alpha and Omega, the Beginning, and the End, the First and the Last. I can do what I want to do. I AM flawless in everything I do. I'm going to show you what a flawless God I am, and everything is done in My timing. A love or promise is worth waiting for, and I will show you through what I am doing. I will talk to you personally throughout this book from time to time because I have a few things to say that I want you to hear.

The story I'm going to share with you is about a husband and wife, Raymond, and Victoria, who desperately want a child. I made them a promise, and they think I have forgotten about them. Raymond is 34 years old, and Victoria is 33. I told them when they were about 23 years old, they would have a son. Victoria thought it was not possible because she was barren due to Me closing her womb. There is nothing wrong with her, but she believes the doctors when they say she has a problem. It has nothing to do with that; I have not opened her womb yet. They have spent a lot of money going to doctors and taking fertility pills. Nothing has happened, and I will not let it because it is not the right time.

Victoria convinced Raymond to ask her sister to be a surrogate mother for her and Raymond. Niriya, her sister, agreed to be the surrogate mother. However, Victoria noticed that Raymond and Niriya were getting quite comfy with one another. Niriya wouldn't leave them alone after she had the baby. Raymond was in tune with his son, Nigel. He didn't pay Niriya any mind. He just loved his son even though he knew in his heart Nigel wasn't the promised son.

Around four years later, after convincing Niriya to be their surrogate, having the baby, and staying longer than expected, Victoria couldn't take it anymore. She hated to see her husband have a bond with any other woman because of a child, even if it was her sister. Niriya became nasty towards Victoria during the pregnancy. Niriya was already staying with them because they wanted to make sure she had the best care and was safe because she lived in the projects and couldn't get "footing" on life. She took advantage of the situation. Whenever Victoria would ask Niriya about the baby, she would become nasty and short answered with her. Niriya told her one time, "This ain't your baby so stop asking me about him." Victoria is not a mean woman; to the contrary, she is a very giving lady. She wanted a son so bad she was willing to take all the scorn Niriya could give. Victoria never thought her own sister would do this to her because, at one time, they were awfully close. When Victoria finally had enough, she told Niriya off, which turned into a huge argument. Niriya left…well, was paid to leave. She told Niriya, "He ain't my promised son anyway. Nigel was never mine, to begin with."

Raymond was hurt to wake up the next morning to find out his son was gone. He asked Victoria where Niriya went with Nigel. She told him she did not know and continued saying, you know how she is, here today and gone tomorrow. Raymond couldn't believe it. His heart was in pain as he mourned for his son. He spent years looking for Nigel but couldn't find him. Niriya never mentioned where she was going. Victoria didn't care to know until she started feeling guilty. Niriya reached out to Victoria to blackmail her into giving more money every month, or she was going to tell Raymond. Niriya had enough money to relocate with the money her sister gave her, set up for a nice place to live, and move on with her life separate from her sister. Now more than ever, he longed for his son promised to him by Me. Victoria is tore up on the inside, keeping from Raymond what really happened between her and Niriya. Ten and a half years have passed since this happened, and Victoria has held onto this secret the whole time. Nigel is fourteen years old now, and Victoria is ready to come clean. She's not coming clean on her own. She's forced to because of extreme guilt, her marriage being on the rocks, nothing is working out for her, and she's still not pregnant. I sent a prophet to her just like I did David. Niriya is on her way back, and she's ready to kick up some dirt.

Guilt Ridden

As Victoria was setting the table for dinner, Raymond noticed she was preoccupied with deep thoughts, and he asked her, "Victoria, what are you thinking about?"

"Let me get my thoughts together, and I will tell you in a minute," she said.

"Are you sure you don't want to tell me now because you look like something is really bothering you," Raymond said.

"Yes, I'm sure…but," Victoria said with a sigh as she signaled for Raymond to come and sit down at the table for dinner.

"But what," he asked?

"Uh, Uhm, Raymond, I don't know how to tell you this," she said.

"Just come on out and say it. Whatever it is, we can make it through it," he said reassuring her.

"I have held on to this for so many years…," she started to say as Raymond cut her off.

"Does this have to do with my son Nigel," he firmly asked.

"Yes, Raymond," she answered shamefully.

"What did you do," he asked as he was getting upset.

"I paid Niriya to take her and Nigel far away and to leave me and you alone," she said.

"You did what," he said as he slammed his hands on the table and got up from his chair, slamming it up against the table.

"Raymond, I'm sorry. I know I should have told you, but…" she said sorrowfully.

"I knew it! I knew something else had happened other than what you told me. What possessed you to do something like that? Victoria, tell me," he said.

"I'm sorry, Raymond. I am so sorry. I know I should have told you, and I never should have done it in the first place. I just couldn't take it anymore," she said as she cried.

"Couldn't take what anymore, Victoria," he asked as he paced back and forth.

"Niriya was spiteful and just mean. You couldn't see she was trying to get to you; all you could see was Nigel. It's not your fault, but I became jealous that God would open her womb and not mine. Then, on top of that, Niriya would make fun of me and torment me. I know it's not an excuse, but I grew tired of it all," she said, becoming angry once more.

"Why didn't you tell me that was going on? I could have fixed it from the get-go," he said.

"I tried telling you, but you didn't want to hear it. All you wanted was the son that I couldn't give you," she said.

"I have not seen Nigel in ten and a half years. Since he was 4, Victoria! Four!" he said as he punched a wall in the dining room.

"All I can say is…I'm sorry, Raymond, and ask you to forgive me."

"I don't know, Victoria. Forgiving you ain't in me. I can't even see how we are going to get past this."

Raymond started to walk out of the dining room, and Victoria got up and ran to him, grabbing his arm and said, "Please, don't say that. We can make it through this." Raymond yanked away from her quietly and kept walking. Then she said in a rushed voice, looking to find something that would stop him in his tracks, "I know where he lives, and I have been sending money to him every month since they left, and I have some pictures of him."

Raymond turned around inflamed, grabbed her arms, stared in her eyes, and said, "You mean to tell me you knew where he was this whole time!" He let her arms go and continued saying, "I asked you if you knew where he was, and you told me you didn't know.

"I didn't know at first. The only way I found out was because she wrote a letter saying I better give her more money or else she was going to tell you what I did."

"So, let me get this straight…you lied, embezzled my money for child support, *and* sent him away?"
Victoria was speechless. He waited for her to answer to say something, anything but she was without words.
Upon seeing Victoria's nonreaction to his question, he said, "Man, I'm out, and I don't know if I'm coming back," Raymond said as he grabbed his keys and walked towards the door."

"Wait! Wait!" Victoria cried as she went to the closet and pulled out some pictures that were in a secret compartment, then continued to say, "Here."

He stopped as she gave him the pictures and fell against the wall while sliding to the floor and said as he gazed upon the photos, "My son."

Raymond gazed upon the photo with relief, pain, and anguish that it moved Victoria to tears, and she finally recognized the severity of what she'd done. She knew she needed to repent and was ready to deal with whatever consequences. He asked her one more question, "Where is my son?"

"He's in Los Angeles."

"I need an address and a phone number. I am going to see my son. I will talk to you when I return. Don't call me."

"Raymond, come back and sit down so we can talk about this."

"We have nothing left to talk about," he said as he walked upstairs to pack some clothes.

"Don't walk out on me, Raymond! I said I was sorry."

He turned around in disgust and said, "That just won't cut it anymore. There have been too many lies for ten years, ten years! I don't want to talk to you about this anymore, at least for right now." He hated to see his wife cry, but his pain was greater. He couldn't deny how much he loves her and is the only reason he's stayed this long in the marriage, even after all they've been through, but he wasn't sure they could get through this hurdle. It was just too much.

"I know I messed up, Raymond, but at least give me the chance to make it right, please, I beg you."

"How can you make this right, Victoria? I need to know."

"I will bring them here, but Niriya will not stay in this house. I can set them up with daddy's house, and you know it won't cost her or us a thing because he left it for her and me. They can stay there. They are welcome at any time to the house, but again she is not allowed to stay here."

"Why don't you want them here."

"Did you not hear anything I said? It's not him who I don't want, but her. This is what I was talking about. All you care about is your son. You could care less about my feelings and what the mother of your son has done to me."

"That is not true. I would never let anyone hurt you, and especially not as bad as you hurt me. Plus, you never said anything, so how was I supposed to know."

"I did mention it to you, but I don't want to go there anymore, but you better believe I cannot let you go to California by yourself. I know Niriya, and she will try to manipulate you, and that is one thing I cannot have."

"You really don't have a choice in this matter, but I'll go along with it. But, I will not be staying in the house until he gets here. Send for Nigel first, though. I want a chance to catch up with him alone," Raymond said as he walked downstairs and out the door to leave for the hotel.

Victoria hated to see what she did to him, especially since he's adamant about not staying at home; therefore, she saw to it immediately to get Nigel back home. She did not wait for one minute. She wanted to show her husband she meant what she said and that she was terribly sorry for what she had done and put him through.

"Hello," Niriya answered the phone.

"Hello, Niriya, it's Victoria," she replied.

"Yeah, what's up," she asked in a rude tone?

"I told Raymond about what happened, so he knows about Nigel and where you live," Victoria said, getting straight to the point.

"It's about time. My child has suffered all these years asking about his father because of you," Niriya said shrewdly.

"I know, and I am deeply sorry for the pain that I caused Nigel and Raymond," Victoria said.

"What about apologizing to me? Have you forgotten that it was you that put me out? What do you have to say for yourself?" Niriya asked.

"You owe me an apology too. I am not sorry for putting you out. I am sorry for putting Nigel out and separating him from his father. As for you, you got what you deserved," Victoria said, firmly standing by her decision.

"You have not changed. I am through talking to you," Niriya said, about to hang up the phone.

"No! Wait!" Victoria pleaded.

"What?" Niriya asked.

"Raymond wants to see Nigel. I told him I would send for the both of you, but he wants to see Nigel first so he can bond with him alone and get reacquainted," she said.

"There are two weeks left before school is out. He can come after that. Where are we supposed to live?" she asked.

"You will stay in daddy's old house. There won't be a mortgage because it is paid off. The house is move-in ready," Victoria said.

"I'm glad you finally came to your senses," Niriya said, hoping to upset her sister some more.

"I don't have time for this. Is Nigel home? I know Raymond wants to talk to him," Victoria said, brushing off the words Niriya just spoke to her.

"Yes, he is right here," she said.

"Put him on the phone. I want to talk to him first and explain what happened, that it was my fault and not to blame his father," Victoria said.

"Don't upset Nigel. You hear me?" Niriya said.

"He is going to be upset with me, but I have to tell him," Victoria said.

"Hold on," said Niriya.

"Hello," Nigel said with a deep voice, wondering what was going on.

"Hi Nigel, this is your aunt Victoria," she said.

"Okay," he said in a nonchalant tone because he didn't remember her.

"I have something to tell you; it's about your father," she said with a lump in her throat.

"What about my father? Do you know where he is?" Nigel asked.

"Yes, I do. He is my husband. I know you have a lot of questions about him, and I am here to answer those questions," she said.

"He's your husband? Awh, that's some backwoods Bama type stuff," he said, disgusted.

"No, it's not what you think," she chuckled.

"What is it then?" he asked.

"I could not have children, so I asked your mother to be a surrogate. She agreed. Then things became very strenuous between your mother and me. After that, I did the unthinkable and asked your mother to leave when you were four years old. I did not tell your father what happened. I blamed it all on your mom. I have been sending money every month to your mom for you since then. She sent pictures of you that I never showed your father. He has longed for you for many years. I want to tell you that I am sorry for the pain I caused you and not to blame your father for what I have done," Victoria said.

"You fa real? Man, that's foul. Do you know…man…bump dis. Mama, take da phone." Nigel said.

"Nigel! Nigel!" Victoria said.

"He don't want to talk no more," Niriya said.

"I just wanted to apologize to him," Victoria said.

"What you think that's supposed to do after over ten years?" Sorry doesn't fix ten years of pain. Sorry doesn't take away the questions he had about his father," Niriya said.

"Ion' want no apology. She can keep dat!" Nigel said yelling in the background.

"Well, all I can do is apologize and try to make things right between the two of them. I will text you Raymond's number since Nigel didn't give me the chance to give it to him," Victoria said.

"What you thought he was just gone let you get off that easy? Girl, bye," Niriya said as she hung up the phone.

Victoria scheduled Nigel's flight as soon as they got off the phone. Once the reservations were made, she sent the details to Raymond, Niriya, and Nigel. At that time, she texted Raymond Niriya's number for him to call Nigel. She thought about giving Niriya Raymond's number but knew that would cause all sorts of other problems.

Afterward, Victoria cried out to me, realizing all the pain she caused her family, "Lord, I am so sorry. I wouldn't blame You if You never opened my womb. I was selfish, and I am sorry. I shouldn't have taken Nigel away from Raymond. I am sorry. I am going to do everything in my power to make this right."

I spoke to Victoria as she prayed and said, "Apologize to Niriya. She was hurt too."

"But Lord, how? What about what she did to me? What about how she treated me?" Victoria asked.

I told her, "I will deal with Niriya about her part. But at this time, I am dealing with you about the role you played in all this."

"I just don't know if I can apologize to her. To be honest with You, I am not sorry about what I said to her. She had it coming. I don't know if I can do that," Victoria said.

"It will not be set right until you do. You are the one that is the role model. You set the tone. It is you who I live in, and there are certain things I expect of you," I told her.

"I will do it, but it is hard," she said as she walked upstairs to her and bedroom.

She heard Raymond come through the front door talking on the phone. "You have no idea how long I have longed to hear your voice. I can't wait to see you in a couple of weeks. When you get here, I am taking a month off work to spend time with you. We have a lot to catch up on," Raymond said to Nigel as he looked past Victoria after walking upstairs.

"After you finish talking to Nigel let me speak to Niriya," Victoria whispered to Raymond, trying not to disturb their moment. He nodded his head to say okay, then quickly returned to his conversation with Nigel.

"What are the kinds of things that you like to do?" he asked Nigel.

"I like to play video games, bowling, and making music," said Nigel.

They talked for a long time, which seemed like hours for Victoria, but she didn't mind. Then Raymond finally told Nigel that he would talk to him later and to put Niriya on the phone.

"Hello Raymond," Niriya said seductively.

"Hi, Victoria wants to speak to you," he said.

"Is that all you have to say?" she replied.

"What do you want me to say? You had just as big of a role in this as my wife," he said as he handed Victoria the phone.

"Niriya, you're right; I owe you an apology. I am sorry for what I did to you. I never should have sent you away, and I am sorry," Victoria said.

"Oh, I get it. Now that you're in front of Raymond, you wanna pretend like you're so sweet and innocent. Chile bye, I ain't even tryin' to hear it," Niriya said.

"Really, Niriya? Is that all you have to say?" Victoria asked.

"Yep, I said all that I have to say. I have to go now. Nigel will be ready in two weeks, and you best believe I will be right behind him. Just make sure you cha' ching me that cash through my app so I can move there," she said as she hung up the phone.

"Ugh…she is so ugh!" Victoria said, upset.

"I hope you don't expect sympathy from me because you will not get it," Raymond said.

"It's cool. I'll take the blows. I'm just glad you're home," Victoria said as she went to hug him.

Raymond pushed her away and said, "Oh, I'm not staying. I had to come back because I forgot something," Raymond said, trying to hurt her just as much as she hurt him.

"Where are you going?" she asked.

"I don't feel like I owe you any explanation. I don't have to tell you nothing," he said rather harshly.

"You know what, I have taken responsibility for what I have done, but I am not going to sit here and continue to take insults from you," she said.

"You'll take whateva I say, and I could care less how you feel about it!" he said and walked out of the room and back out of the house.

Victoria went to bed to forget about what happened and end this bad day. She didn't even try to slip on her silk nightgown with the silk robe to match. Victoria put on her black and red flannel pajamas, wrapped her hair, and put on her infamous "grease rag," as Raymond would call it, to tease her and make her laugh. She tossed and turned for hours because she wondered where Raymond was and what he was doing. Raymond stayed out until the wee hours of the morning on purpose.

He went to the bar across town. Raymond hasn't been in a bar in years since he's been serving Me. However, he found himself driving carelessly to a bar to drown his pain. I know I had to send an angel to help him. His flesh wants to drink and get drunk and lay up with some random woman. He is a handsome man and easy on the eyes. Women come on to him all the time, but the love he has for Victoria surpassed what they were trying to put out. Nevertheless, his spirit is praying to Me for help, but ultimately the decision has to be his.

"What will you be having?" the bartender asked.

"Black Russian," Raymond said like an old pro.

"Alright," the bartender responded.

As the bartender walked away to fix the drink, Raymond put his head in his hands and wondered about Victoria and what she did. A woman from across the room spotted him. She approached Raymond and said, "You look like a man that needs someone to talk to." Raymond replied, "Well, it ain't you, and I've had enough of women today." She rolled her eyes and walked away. Then a man walked in with a shaggy beard, jeans with holes in the knees, a t-shirt, and a clean haircut sat next to Raymond, "Hey, are you alright? You look like you have a lot on your mind," the man said.

"I do," Raymond said.

"Do you want to talk about it?" the man asked.

"No, not really. I don't even know you. I am not in the habit of telling things to people I don't know," Raymond said.

"Here you go, sir," the bartender said as he handed Raymond his drink.

"Thank you," he said.

"Sir, what will you be having," the bartender asked the man.

"I'll have a coke," the man said.

"You got it," the bartender said.

Raymond held on to his drink and looked at the bottom of the glass, contemplating on taking the drink. He continued to be silent as the strange man looked upon him. As he raised his drink to his mouth, the man said, "Is this your first time here?"

"Yes," said Raymond.

"Man, it must be bad for you to end up here with that drink in your hand," he said.

"You don't know the half of it," Raymond responded.

"Days like that I have to get away too," the strange man said.

"Here is your coke," the bartender said.

"Thank you," the man said to the bartender but really concentrating on Raymond.

"Where do you go to get away?" Raymond asked.

"You don't want to know," the stranger answered.

Raymond looked him up and down and said, "Maybe not."

He'd distracted Raymond from taking the drink so far, but as soon as he put the glass to his lip, the stranger said, "Come over and play some pool with us and get your mind off your troubles."

"I don't think so," Raymond said.

"Come on, man. What will it hurt?" the stranger said.

Raymond looked at him and said, "Alright, man. He grabbed his drink and followed the stranger.

They walked to the pool table, and the stranger introduced everyone. He said, "Hey Ham and Sarah, meet…uh…"

"Raymond," he said, introducing himself. "Ham?" Raymond asked.

"It's short for Abraham," Sarah answered.

"Abraham and Sarah? Yeah right. Is this some kind of joke," Raymond asked sarcastically?

"I know it's comical, and believe me when I say we knew what people were going to say when we started dating. My wife and I hear jokes all the time," Ham said.

"Wait until you hear our story. That's really going to freak you out," Sarah said as they all began to laugh.

"What's your story?" Raymond asked.

"We'll get to that later," Sarah said.

"So, what brings you here tonight, Raymond?" Ham asked.

"Nothing I want to talk about," Raymond said.

"I get that," Ham said, laughing.

"Boys, are we going to play, or are we going to talk about our feelings," Sarah said, mocking the men.

"You have to forgive Sarah. She's a little rough around the edges," Caleb, the stranger said, talking about this woman who had the look of a biker chick. They laughed and played a few games of pool. Then they sat down in a booth to eat and talk.

"Awh, he has a laugh," Sarah said.

"Oh, you funny," Raymond said. His phone rang but he didn't answer.

"Not someone you want to talk to, I supposed," Ham said.

"Not at all," Raymond said.

"Oh, you mad, mad then," Sarah said, and they giggled.

"I don't even know how to feel about it," Raymond said.

"Yeah, me and Sarah had them kind of days," Ham said.

"How did y'all get through?" Raymond asked.

"A lotta Jesus," Sarah said.

"I don't know if He'd handle this though," Raymond said.

"We didn't think so either, but He did and now we go around the globe sharing our story," Ham said.

"What's your story?" Raymond asked.

"Sarah was told by the doctors she would never have children, but God made me a promise and told me we would. Man, we waited for years, but before deciding to let God be God, we made the mistake of letting one of her friends be the surrogate mother. She made our lives unbearable. She treated Sarah so bad, like making fun of her, flaunting around her belly, making Sarah feel less than a woman, then started to come after me. To this day, I wish we never done it, but I thank God for my son, nonetheless. After he was born, things became even worse. The chick kept calling me to come over because of something the baby "needed." When I'd get there, nothing was as she said, so I started sending Sarah instead. Sarah was fed up, and she went off on her. Eventually, she left and took my son with her, never saying a word. We still don't know where he is, and I'd like to know, but God blessed us with our promised son, so we're good," Abraham said.

"Man, that's crazy. I know y'all lying," Raymond said.

"Very serious," Sarah said.

"Ain't no way," Raymond said.

"I swear it's like a cruel joke God played on us. From us dating and our names being what they are to the same storyline as in the Bible, it's crazy," Ham said.

"Yeah, that's crazy. My wife and I are going through something similar, except she convinced me to ask her sister to be the surrogate mother, and she agreed. We didn't sleep with each other. She became pregnant by artificial insemination. My sister-in-law had my son, but she stayed around. Then suddenly, my son and his mother were gone without an explanation. My wife didn't seem moved one way or the other. While we were sitting down eating dinner this evening, she tells me she sent her sister away with my son. She always knew where they were and never said a word knowing how long I searched for my son. One thing my wife did was send money for him so he wouldn't have to struggle. That was the least she could do," he said.

Ham was about to speak, but Sarah cut him off. "Ham, it's my turn," Sarah said as she smiled at her husband. She finished saying, "I know what she did was wrong, but did you take the time to look at it from her side?"

"Not really. I just want my son back. That's all I can think about," he said.

"There is no excuse for what she did, but if you would take the time to think about what she went through. It doesn't justify what she did, but it could possibly help you to understand. I am willing to guess your sister-in-law is less than a gem. It sounds like to me you are more worried about your son than your wife. Out that whole process, you forgot about her. I'm not saying to forget about your son, but what I am saying is don't forget about your wife," Sarah said.

"She's right. These problems probably could have been avoided if I focused on her and not put so much emphasis on my son. Her friend was looking for something that I wasn't able to give, and I guarantee that's what your sister-in-law was looking for too," Abraham said.

"I guess you are right. I never really saw it like that," Raymond said.

"I didn't either until God showed me what was really going on. Sarah tried to tell me, but I wasn't listening, and it started to tear us apart. Pray about it, and God will show you what to do. Love on your wife. Don't leave her out in the cold," he said.

"That's going to be hard. I'm not going to lie to you. Hey, where did Caleb go?" Raymond asked.

"He does that all the time. He helps people then disappears on them. It's kind of like his signature," said Sarah.

"I wanted to thank him for helping me and encouraging me not to drink. It was because of him I didn't take a sip of that Black Russian. He was easy to talk to, and I do not usually spill my guts to strangers," he said.

"He knows you appreciate it. It's what he does. Well, it's been good talking to you. I hope we helped," said Abraham.

"Yes, you did, but I don't think anybody will believe this story," said Raymond.

They all laughed and said their good-byes. Raymond turned his head for a minute, and when he looked for them, Ham and Sarah were gone as if they had disappeared too.

Raymond paid for his drink and food then left the bar. He checked into a hotel and stayed there for a week. He didn't talk to Victoria at all. He needed time to clear his head. I allowed it because it was warranted. I didn't expect him to go back home and act like nothing happened. Raymond needed his space. He should have spoken to Victoria though, but I let it slide.

Meanwhile, Victoria was at home lost. It killed her on the inside not knowing where her husband stayed. She called but he'd never answer. She was sure he was with another woman. Victoria didn't know what to think, but now she could understand how her husband felt when he didn't know where his son lived.

While Raymond was trying to decide what he was going to do about his marriage, and remembering Ham and Sarah, he thought to himself, "God, I don't know what you are doing, but I have no choice but to follow your plan." He made up his mind to go home to his wife.

The day he decided to come home, he stayed late at work. He knew he was taking some time off, so he got ahead start on some work. He also stayed late to punish Victoria. She was already in bed for the night and not expecting Raymond to come home. She heard him moving around in the bedroom but pretended like she was still sleeping. He got in bed and went to sleep. He heard Victoria sniffling but didn't want to ask what was wrong because he didn't care. She tried to keep it under wraps, but it became too much, so Raymond asked her, "What is wrong, Victoria? Why are you crying?"

"Nothing, it's alright. Just go to sleep," she replied.

"No, I will not just go to sleep. I want to know what is wrong with you," he pushed.

"You have been gone for a week nor answered or returned any of my calls."

"You lucky cause I wasn't coming back at all."

"But you say that all the time when we argue, but you always come home. Thoughts have been running through my head, is all. I just want to go to sleep," she said.

"Victoria, you don't have anything to worry about. At first, I was going to be cruel and make you think I did something and let you wonder about that for ten years. Still, something happened to me this past week," he said as he laid on his back, looking at the ceiling.

"What happened?" she asked.

"Nothing, go to sleep. We'll talk in the morning."

"Tell me what happened."

"Just know that something happened, and you ought to be glad it did," he said.

"Uhm," Victoria snorted.

They went to sleep. Raymond slept peacefully, but Victoria tossed and turned. Neither one of them said goodnight to each other, nor did they say, "I love you," as they do every night. This bothered Victoria, but she was just grateful he came home.

Raymond woke up the next morning and got himself ready for work. He went downstairs to see if there was any breakfast made, but there was nothing ready. In the mornings, he usually smells bacon frying, pancakes, coffee brewing, and whatever else Victoria would fix him in the morning before going to work, but to his dismay, there wasn't any of that going on this morning. Victoria left without saying a word. She didn't give him his kisses, nor did she give Raymond a chance to give his to her. He was bothered. "Why is Victoria like this?" he wondered. "If anyone should have been mad, it should be me."

He walked out of the house hungry, puzzled, and a bit upset. This is how he had to start his day. However, little did he know Victoria was on her way to making things right with her household. She made a whole day of it. Victoria didn't call Raymond all day. He couldn't concentrate at work, and there was a big production he was producing. His long-time friend walked up to him in the hallway because he could tell that his friend had a lot on his mind.

"Hey man, what's going on with you today? You haven't been yourself for about a week. I wanted to ask, but it didn't seem like a good time, so I left you be," Joshua said.

"It's nothing, man. How is the production coming along?" Raymond asked, avoiding the subject.

"Everything is fine. It will be okay, but I am more concerned about you. You my boi; I know you, and I can always tell when something is going on with my pat'na. Tell me. What's up?" he asked again.

"Let's go to my office because I don't want ears to hear this," Raymond said.

As they quietly walked down the hallway, Raymond was thinking about a way to tell his friend about everything that happened. They stepped into his office, and Raymond said, "Can you close the door for me?"

"Sure," Joshua said, closing the door.

"Do you remember my son Nigel?" Raymond asked him.

"Yeah, the surrogate mother thing, the one by your sister-in-law, right?" Joshua said, making sure.

"Yes, that one," Raymond said.

"Well, what about him? I mean, whatever happened to him," Joshua asked.

"I told you his mother took him and left," Raymond continued as Joshua nodded his head in a yes response, "Well, I found out yesterday that is not true. Victoria told me she sent them away."

"What!" Joshua said.

"Yeah, man. She sent my son away," Raymond said.

"Why did she do that?" he asked.

"She said Niriya was mistreating her, and she was trying to get close to me, and she became fed up. She also said that I wasn't noticing what was going on; that I was all into Nigel instead of paying attention to what was happening in our home," he said as his nostrils flared up. "Why are you making that face?" Raymond asked Joshua because he had a look like "I told you so."

"Because man, I told you Niriya was a bad idea. We've known her since they moved in the hood at middle school, and you know how she was. A ghetto bird if we ever saw one. It was only a matter of time before it all hit the fan. You should have waited on God. I told you!"

"I know, but Victoria insisted. You know how she can be."

"That has never stopped you from telling her no before. Anyway, where does that leave you and Victoria?"

"She is doing everything she can to fix things, but I don't know."

"What is it that you don't know about? This is Victoria. She made a mistake. This woman has been by you through everything, and I do mean everything. It's jacked up what she did, but she really didn't have to tell you. Dawg, it's a mistake."

"It's not that easy. Nobody seems to understand, it's not that easy."

"I never said it was easy, but I am telling you it was a mistake. She owned up to it and is trying to make things right. Can you really say that it wouldn't have ended up like this anyway? I mean, seriously, we're talking about Niriya. There ain't nothing good about that girl. Everywhere she went, she caused problems. Victoria ain't the only one who did this, so did Niriya. She didn't tell you either, so are you going to go after her with the same hostility like you are with Victoria? I don't hear you saying Niriya is trying to make things right, but at least Victoria is."

Raymond paused and said, "Victoria is bringing them back down here. They have been in California all this time. Niriya has been sending pictures that I never got. Victoria was sending money to her for Nigel and paid her to leave when she left. Victoria left this morning without saying a word nor cooking a breakfast."

"Wow, that's heavy. Well, at least she did send money. She has kept this a secret for what…almost ten years?"

"Yeap, it has been ten years since I saw my son. I don't know what he looks like or anything, but I did get to talk to him yesterday."

"Really, how was that?"

"It was great. I can't wait to see him. Even though I got to talk to him, I'm still mad as I don't know what with Victoria. I don't even want to be around her. After this went down last week, I thought I was going to be alright, but I just don't know."

"All I'm saying is, don't think too long. Don't give the devil any room to play. You know he will try to make this worse than what it already is, and y'all don't need that."

"I hear you."

"I know you do, but I want you to listen. There is a difference. It will be a long road because this is hard for you, but while traveling this road, do not lose your wife in the process. The love of your son and the neglect of your wife has already put a strain on your marriage and the relationship with your son. Don't let the same love for your son, and the anger with Victoria totally destroy your marriage and everything you love."

"I thought you were my friend. Aren't you supposed to be on my side? Everybody seems to be taken her side. I'm the one that was wronged. Why does everyone think the man is the one who has to make all the changes and sacrifice?"

"Bro, would you like some cheese to go with that whine, and who is everybody? Man up, dawg."

"People from the bar."

"People, huh?"

"I met some people at the bar the night I found out, and they told me their story, and I am not going to get into all that with you because you wouldn't believe me if told you."

"I understand you mad with me, and it's cool. I am your friend, and a true friend wouldn't have told you anything differently."

"You do not understand! You don't understand the hurt, the pain, the longing…and even after all this time, Victoria and I still haven't had a baby of our own though God said we would."

"You're right. I don't get it, but I know you, and I know you still love Victoria."

"I do still love her."

Raymond's secretary beeped in on the phone, and he told Joshua to hold on and answered the call, "Yes, Mrs. Steppleton."

"Mr. Logan is on line one," she said.

"Could you please take a message? I'm in a meeting right now, thank you," he said.

She said, "Yes, sir," as she hung the phone.

"Raymond, you are going to be alright. You will make it through this. Let God be the one who fixes it, not you, not Victoria, but God. When He does it, all really will be well."

"Thanks, man. I don't want to talk about it anymore. I'm drained. Let's get back to work."

"Good because I am ready to get this movie finished."

They went back to work. Raymond was still bothered because he hadn't heard from Victoria. He tried calling her a few times during the day, but she wouldn't answer her phone. The workday ended, and Raymond was on his way home. He looked for Victoria's car but didn't see it.

After he arrived home, took a shower, read the Bible, and prayed, then Victoria walked through the door. She had bags upon bags in her hands.

"Victoria, where have you been? I have tried to call you all day," he asked.

"I went shopping.

"Is that all you have to say for yourself? You went shopping. You can't be serious. Where do you get off leaving early in the morning without so much as a goodbye? On top of that, you don't even answer your phone. I want more of an explanation other than you went shopping."

"First of all, calm down. Check yourself. I didn't want you to know I left this morning because I wanted to surprise you. I figured you could at least fix or buy yourself some breakfast while I went to do what I planned to do. I didn't want to answer the phone because I didn't want to tell you where I was or what I was doing. Now, would you like to hear and see what I was doing?"

"Go ahead."

"How about you unfold your arms and help me bring in this stuff."

"What's all this? How am I supposed to feel about you going out and spending money like this?"

While Raymond helped her bring the bags inside the house, Victoria began to tell him about her day. She told him, "I called Pastor this morning to see if I could meet with him and Co-Pastor today, and he said yes. We meet for lunch, and I told them everything that happened."

"Everything?"

"Everything, from beginning to end, from then, up until now. Of course, I got scolded by him and Co-Pastor, but I expected that. After they lit into me, they helped me sort out some things. I had to take a real good look at myself. I'm not perfect. I do make mistakes, but they told me I would have to be patient with you, which is understandable. I do not expect you to forgive me right away, and it's okay. I will give you your space, but amid that, I will make it easy for you to love and trust me again.

"Victoria, I love you, I do. It's the trust issue that we have to deal with…" he said, but she cut him off.

"My question to you is, are you willing to do whatever it takes to make it work?" she asked.

"Yes, I am, but that's a question I should be asking you. I'm not the one who did wrong."

"I promise you I am going to do everything in my power to show you that you can trust me."

"Now, tell me, what is all this?"

"I know Nigel will be here in a couple of weeks, and I wanted you to be ready for him. All of this is for him. I want to turn one of the guest bedrooms into his room. Here are the bed linens and comforter. I bought him this game console and games to go with it. The television is still in the trunk of the car. I bought two of everything, one for here and the other for mom and dad's house for his room there. Nigel has some gift certificates just in case he doesn't like the clothes I bought for him. Here are a couple of fishing rods for you and him with the accessories. I planned a fishing trip for you two when he gets here."

After a few seconds, Raymond paused then put a huge smile on his face. He walked toward her and gave her the biggest hug. Then he said, "Thank you, Victoria. Thank you."

She melted in his arms. Victoria longed to have her husband to hug her like this for so long. Ever since she sent Nigel away, Raymond didn't give her the affection he once did. As he held her, she laid her head on his shoulders, closed her eyes, and a tear fell to the floor. When her tear hit the floor, it sounded like water dripping from a faucet into a sink full of water. This was the beginning of restoration, or so she thought.

Return of the Son

For her, it has been heaven since Victoria had come clean about Nigel three and a half weeks ago. He is flying in today. Raymond is so happy that he doesn't know what to do with himself. Victoria realizes it's not going to be about her when he gets here. There is a lot of time to make up for, and she is nervous, though, because she doesn't know how Nigel will take her. She waited at home, trying to make sure everything was perfect while Raymond picks up Nigel from the airport.

Raymond looked on the Arrival board to see what gate Nigel's plane would land. He is so happy-nervous that he doesn't know his right from his left. He has made three wrong turns, and he finally stopped to ask a clerk. He heard the announcer say, "Flight 3242 is now landing."

"Oh, my God. That's his flight," Raymond said.

"Calm down, sir. May I help you?" the clerk asked.

And before you knew it, Raymond blurted out to the clerk, "I haven't seen my son since he was four years old. That was ten years ago, and now he is coming in on this flight, and I don't know how to get to him."

"Congratulations! I will take you where his baggage will arrive. You are too excited, and personally, I don't think you would find him on your own," the attendant said.

They walked a few more minutes and arrived at the baggage claim area. Raymond got there the same time Nigel was coming down the escalator. Raymond stared at Nigel from afar for a slow, staggering ten seconds. He recognized him from the pictures Victoria gave him. Nigel knew who his father was because it was like looking in the mirror.

"Well, Sir, you are here. Stop standing around. Go find him and hug him," the attendant said.

"Oh yeah, you're right. Thank you," Raymond said in a scared voice.

Raymond and Nigel approached each other and stood there for seemed like an eternity. Nobody knew what was going on. All they saw were two men staring at each other. They didn't know whether to duck, dodge, or stay still. Then they tried to shake hands because they were too "manly" to cry. Suddenly, Raymond pulled Nigel to him, hugged him, and wouldn't let him go. People in the airport watching this didn't know what was going on, and the attendant said, "That is his son. He hasn't seen him in ten years." The people said, "Ohhhh. Awwwwh," and began clapping and recording with their smartphones.

"Ooh, you have no idea of how much I've missed you," Raymond said to Nigel.

Nigel really didn't know how to act, but he was glad to meet his father. They grabbed Nigel's bags and headed for home. Then Raymond asked Nigel, "Are you hungry?"

"Yeah, that food on the plane sucked," he said.

Raymond wasn't pleased with being answered by a nonchalant "yeah" from a teenager, but he realized who his momma was, so he let it slide. He understood it wouldn't be a good idea to jump down his throat about it, so instead, he said, "How's your mother doing?"

"She really wanted to come, but she's good," he said.

"Well, she'll be here in a couple of weeks. I just wanted some alone time with you. Is that alright?" he asked.

"Yeah, I mean, I really don't know you like that but I want to get to know you. Is your wife going to be around?" Nigel asked in a smart teenager way.

"Victoria apologized for what she's done and knows that these two weeks are about you and me. She even went as far as to make fishing trip arrangements for us."

"It's the least she could do. I know that is your wife, but I ain't feelin' her. All I know is she took you away from me, and I had to grow up without you."

"I understand…because she did take you away, and I haven't forgiven her, but Victoria is a good person. She just made a big mistake. In time we'll both forgive her."

"Hey, man, I don't know about all of that."

"Just give it time."

"Whateva, yo."

All this slang and disrespect was getting under Raymond's skin, but he kept his cool. "Where do you want to eat?" he asked Nigel.

"I like Chinese food."

"I have the perfect spot."

"Can I call my mom to tell her that I made it?"

"Here," Raymond said, handing Nigel the cell phone.

While Nigel was calling his mother, Raymond was praying in his mind, "Lord, I thank You. I really thank You for this opportunity to rebuild my relationship with my son. Father, you heard my cry, and I thank You. I'm going to do everything right too. Lead me on how to win him. I can't undo everything that his mother and my wife did, but I can put him into Your hands for You to raise him. Thank you."

"Here," Nigel said handing Raymond the phone.

"How is she doing?"

"Ask her for yourself," Nigel said making Raymond realize she was still on the phone. "She wants to talk to you," he continued.

"Hello," Raymond said.

"Long time no hear from," Niriya said.

"How have you been?" Raymond asked.

"I've been fine, but I could have been better if Victoria would have let you be there for our son," she said.

"Yeah, but I'm going to tell you like I told Nigel, Victoria came clean, apologized, and had been going over and beyond to make things right," Raymond said.

"Still protecting her, huh? It's the least she could do."

"I'm not doing this with you. I just wanted to know how you were.

"That's a'ight. She may be your wife, but I have your son."

"You have a good day," Raymond said, ending the conversation with her and hanging up the phone.

They went out to eat and had a good time. Victoria was waiting for them to get home. She prepared for Nigel to come to the house, and she was nervous. Victoria doesn't know what to expect when he comes through the door. However, she isn't naïve. She knows Nigel will have anything but warm fuzzy feelings for her. Victoria begins to pray, "Father, I need your help. I know I messed up and messed up big time. Again, I'm sorry for what I've done. Let these two weeks be a blessing to us all and not turmoil in the name of Jesus. I need your help. I can't do this on my own."

Just as she was praying, Raymond and Nigel walked in, "Hey Victoria! We're here!" Raymond yelled upstairs because he didn't see her downstairs.

"I'm on my way down!" Victoria yelled back as she got herself together and went downstairs.

"Where is the bathroom?" Nigel asked, wanting to avoid meeting his auntie.

"Go down the hall, and it's the second door on your left," Raymond said.

Nigel walked off to the bathroom, and Victoria walked downstairs and asked Raymond, "Where is he?"

"He went to the bathroom," Raymond said.

"How was your afternoon?" she asked.

"Long overdue, and loved every minute of it," Raymond said

"That's good. I'm not going to stand in y'all way. After I see him, then I will leave," she said.

"You don't have to leave. In fact, I'd prefer you to stay. Regardless of what went on, we are family, and it's not going to get any easier running and hiding. We are going to make it through this," he said as he lifted up her head with his pointer finger, making her look him in his eyes, and continued saying, "As a family."

Victoria looked at Raymond and smiled. Then, Nigel walked up, and Raymond said, "Nigel, this is your aunt Victoria."

"Hey," Nigel said, sounding detached.

"Hi," Victoria said, extending her arm.

Nigel just looked at her hand and then at her and said, "Dad, where is my room?"

"Nigel, I'm not going to have you disrespecting my wife. I know you don't like what she did, but I can't have you disrespecting my wife and in my house."

"Raymond, it's okay. I knew it wouldn't be easy for him."

"Whateva man. Can I please just go to my room?"

"Come on. I will take you to your room. I'm not saying you have to be fake but at least be cordial," Raymond said.

"Look, man, I didn't ask to come here. My momma should have come, and I wouldn't have to stay here," Nigel said.

"Raymond, it's okay; it's going to take some getting used to. Go and have fun with your son. I will be at Leigha's house," Victoria said.

"Victoria, you don't have to leave," Raymond said.

"I know you and Nigel need spend some time together, and I will see you later on tonight," Victoria said, getting her keys to the Benz and walking out the door.

"Nigel, we are going to have to talk," Raymond said.

"'Bout what?" Nigel questioned.

"I know you are angry with Victoria, and you don't like her, but I can't have you running my wife out of her own house. I'm not asking you to fall all over her and revere her. All I'm asking is that you be respectful. She will have to earn your trust and love one day at a time, and she realizes that. Are we understood?" Raymond said.

"I got you," Nigel said.

"So that means we are going to enjoy these couple of weeks, right?" Raymond asked.

"I told you, man, I got you," Nigel said.

"Come on and let me show you to your room," Raymond said.

They went up the decorated stairs, down the hall to the last door, and Raymond opened the door. Nigel said, trying to play it cool but screaming on the inside, "This is straight."

"Go on and get relaxed. I'm going to get a shower," Raymond said.

"Where is the bathroom up here?" Nigel asked.

"It is attached to your bedroom, right here," Raymond said as he showed him.

"Awh man, you playin' me," Nigel said excitedly.

"Naw, I ain't playin' you. This is real, son," Raymond said in a New York accent.

Nigel started laughing and said, "A'ight."

"I'll be back after I get my shower," Raymond said.

His father left and Nigel had a blast in his room, as cool as a teenager could be. He made himself at home. After everything calmed down and they spent some more time together, they headed off to bed, but Victoria was still gone. Raymond was concerned about her but knew she would be home later, or at least she better be.

Meanwhile, at Victoria's friend Leigha's house, they were talking. "Girl, I know I was wrong, so I will deal with all the drama," Victoria said.

"Yeah, you were, but you don't have to take disrespect either, but his respect is something that you will have to earn," Leigha said.

"I don't know what to expect when my sister gets here, though. She was just as wrong as I was, but she places all the blame on me," Victoria said.

"I still can't figure out why you used her as a surrogate anyway. That was crazy. You know how she is," Leigha said.

"It's too late now. I have to deal with it," said Victoria.

"So, what are you going to do?" Leigha asked.

"Just staying out of the way," Victoria responded.

"Is that really the answer?" Leigha asked.

"I don't know, Leigha, all I can do is what I think is best, and that is to stay out of the way," Victoria said.

"But how is Raymond going to feel about that?"

"Who knows, I believe part of him wouldn't mind. I couldn't tell you."

"I know I'm not in your situation, but what I think I would do is to spend time with them bit by bit, maybe not being so overwhelming but integrating day by day."

"I might do that, but Leigha, I don't even know how to speak to Nigel. I can't communicate with him."

"He will come around. Don't worry about that."

"I'm trying not to."

Leigha and Victoria continued to talk for the rest of the night. They laughed at movies and ate ice cream with cheesecake. The women had a "golden girls" moment. Victoria felt a little better about what was going on at home. She rested her mind and thoughts.

"I think it's time for me to go home before Raymond gets worried."

"It is kind of late. I mean, what would ol' Mr. Raymond do if his wife came in after one something in the morning?

"You need to stop."

"I betcha he texted you, didn't he?"

"Nooo…"

"Yeah, he did," Leigha said laughing, then continued saying, "Ya boy has stalker-like tendencies."

"Whatever, Leigha," Victoria said, laughing because she knew Raymond had texted her. But she was not about to give Leigha the satisfaction of being right.

"You betta get home or else."

"I'm going, but before I do, since you are all up in mine, how are things going with you and 'ol boy? And when will I finally meet him?"

"I'on know. I don't think I'm gone keep homie around. You know I don't do that "saved" thing. I don't know how I keep meeting these Christian men cause I'm trying to stay far away from them. Bruh man ain't givin' it up either, and you know I gots to get mine," Leigha said.

"You need to get saved."

"And do what? Be up in church all day, lifting holy hands and whatnot, gurl, I ain't trying to settle down with him nor Jesus right now," Leigha said laughing and mocking.

"You are crazy. I don't even know why I hang with you. The Bible says not to be unequally yoked, and I think our friendship has passed that boundary," Victoria said laughing also.

"Whateva. Somebody betta, tell ya boy to give it up and let me see what I'm working with before we continue any further," Leigha said, rolling her eyes and pointing her finger as we know how some black females do.

"Get saved."

"I'm gone see Jesus, just not today."

"Anyway, I'm going now, and I'll talk to your crazy butt tomorrow."

"Alright, girl, you know I love you, and I'm here if you need me."

"Thanks a lot for everything. Bye," Victoria said and waved goodbye, leaving Leigha's house.

Victoria dreaded going home because she knew she'd have to explain to Raymond how come she had been gone for so long. There is no way that she wants to talk about the situation further. Victoria is hoping when she gets home, Nigel is asleep, but she already knows Raymond won't sleep until she is in the house. While Victoria was on her way home, Raymond paced the floor because this wasn't like his wife to walk through their door at almost two in the morning, and she was not answering her texts. He is really worried about her and mad too. Finally, Victoria arrives home, and Raymond lets her have it.

"So, you don't know how to answer calls or texts?"

"I was over Leigha's watching movies and talking."

"What that got to do with you answering my calls. And I know you crazy thinking you just gone walk in my house at this time of night. What's up with that?"

"Well, hello to you too."

"Don't hello me. You better start talking."

"Where do you think I've been? I told you I was going to Leigha's for a while to give you and Nigel some space."

"Space is something you put between words, not a marriage. It's cool that you wanted to give us some time together, but I told you that you didn't have to go anywhere. Victoria, this is your house."

"I know."

"I want us to learn to live as a family."

"Live as a family? What are you saying?"

"We have to learn to live as a family because Nigel is here for good, and Niriya will be here in a matter of weeks. You, me, and Nigel have to learn to bear with one another before she gets here."

"I guess, but can we talk about this in the morning. I'm tired right now."

"Yeah, come on upstairs, and I'll bring you some hot tea."

"Thank you."

"Anyway, today was one of the happiest days of my life. You could say I have a new outlook on life. I realized today that life is too short to spend it mad and angry with someone that you genuinely love when God can restore what was lost in a day, and today God did that for me."

"Uhm, mm…" Victoria mummed.

"What was that about?" Raymond asked.

"Oh, nothing, just thinking. I'm going upstairs now," Victoria said.

"I'll meet you up there," Raymond said.

Victoria got herself ready for bed, awaiting Raymond with the hot tea. He was happy his wife was home, and he got to see his son. Raymond is on cloud nine. The next morning when Victoria woke up, she heard jazz music throughout the house. She even smelled breakfast cooking. Now, this was new to her because although Raymond is a good man, brotha man doesn't cook. Victoria got up, put on her robe, and walked down the stairs, not knowing what else to expect. She didn't see Nigel, so the morning was good for her so far. Victoria walked into the kitchen, gazing at her husband in awe. Sitting here was a fine specimen of a man, drenched in a Steve Darbey suit from head to toe, smelling good with a hint of Burberry cologne, and a breakfast table set for two. He is sitting at one end, and her plate is cata-cornered to his with a rose lying across her plate.

"My God!" Victoria screamed in her head while her facial expression is telling every little thing she's thinking. "Is everything alright?" Raymond asked, knowing he just laid it down.

"Uh…yes," Victoria responded.

"The look on your face says it all," Raymond said with a grin.

"I mean…wow…this is fabulous. May I sit?" she asked cordially.

Raymond pushed back his chair, and stood up, walked over to her chair, pulled it out for her, and said, "Sit my queen."

Victoria pulled together both sides of her silk, laced V-neck, baby blue nightgown outlined in white sequenced lace with the robe to match to sit down properly. Then Raymond pushed her chair up to the table. The setting was beautiful. It had various colorful fruits, lightly buttered toasts, Belgian waffles (her favorite), sunny-side-up eggs with apple juice, and a caramel latte.

"Sweetheart, whatever you want, go ahead and get it," Raymond said.

Truthfully, Victoria wanted to dive into it, but she contained herself. She didn't want Raymond to know that he did his thing. The couple ate their food. This was turning out to be the most wonderful morning. After they finished eating, Nigel came downstairs, and he seemed to have turned a glorious moment into a horror movie.

"Well, good morning, son," Raymond said.

"What's up," Nigel responded.

"No, the proper response is good morning," Raymond said.

"My bad…good morning," Nigel sarcastically responded.

"We are going to have a good day today," Raymond said.

"Would you like something to eat, Nigel?" Victoria asked.

"Naw, I'm a'ight," Nigel said.

Raymond cut his eyes at Nigel and said, "I am only going to tell you one more time. Re-Spect my wife."

"Look, man, I didn't come here for all of this," Nigel said.

"Hey, everybody, just chill out! Nigel, if you don't want to eat, that's fine, and Raymond, he knows I am your wife. Baby, he needs time," Victoria said.

"Nigel, go upstairs and get yourself ready for the day so we can go out," Raymond said.

"Whateva man," Nigel said.

Nigel went upstairs and ruined her good morning. Victoria felt worse than she did the night before. Raymond and Nigel spent the day together, but Nigel has a bad attitude and talked about going back to be with his mom. Raymond is trying everything to get him to stay and to stick things out.

As they are sat down eating at a fast-food restaurant, Raymond said, "Nigel, how about we work on the house for your mom together?"

"Man, I don't mean no harm, but I don't want to be around your wife," he said.

"I understand how you feel, but you got to accept the fact that my wife is going to be around. She is doing her best to stay out of your way…if you hadn't noticed."

"As she should."

"I was upset too, but we have already been through all this."

"Yeah, but it doesn't mean that I have to get over it all of a sudden."

"True, but you don't have to make it hard either.

"I guess not."

"So, can we at least work on the house for your mom together?"

"I guess so."

"Don't look like it's going to kill you to do it."

"You're asking a lot."

"I know, but just trust me, Nigel."

"A'ight, but can we talk about something else?"

"Sure. What do you want to talk about?"

"I 'on know…just anything but that." Nigel and Raymond talked about other things. Raymond was just excited to be able to get to know his son better.

Sin Repercussions

As time went on and Niriya's arrival was drawing nigh, they all worked on the house together to get ready for Nigel's mother. Victoria enjoyed working with the guys to get the house ready. Nigel didn't want to admit it, but he did too. As they were painting the house, Victoria accidentally splattered some paint on Nigel.

"Oh! I'm sorry, Nigel. I didn't mean…," Victoria said in fear of what he might say and do.

"Yes, you did," Nigel responded in his same old mean tone.

Victoria held her head down and went back to painting. Then suddenly, she was splattered with red paint all in her hair. Raymond watched all this from afar. He didn't want to get in the middle of it, mainly because he didn't see any harm in it.

"Oh! I'm sorry," Nigel said with a smile waiting for Victoria to retaliate.

"In my hair! In my hair! You know how black women are about their hair, and you chose to put paint in my hair!" Victoria shouted. Raymond didn't know what to do at this point because he knew how she felt about her hair. He was in the corner too scared to come out of it. Even Nigel didn't know how to take it. Poor thing had a frightened look on his face too.

"Victoria…," Raymond said hesitantly.

"Oh, no! I don't care what you say. Nigel is going to get it!" Victoria smiled, took a can of paint, and poured it on Nigel's clothes.

Victoria and Nigel signaled each other and walked over to Raymond, who was trying to stay out of it and poured paint on him.

"Y'all couldn't just keep this between the both of you," Raymond said in a threatening tone.

"What you gone do, BIG MAN," Nigel said.

"This!" Raymond responded by taking a paint roller pin and rolling paint on Nigel's face.

They continued to make a mess of the house they were supposed to be cleaning up, but I know what I'm doing in their lives. They all needed this, especially Victoria. She was walking on eggshells to please Nigel and Raymond. I had to let her know that everything was going to be alright.

After the fun festivities, they cleaned up the mess, then themselves up, went out to eat, and enjoyed one another's company. Victoria felt so at peace, more so than she has in a long time. She knows it will still take some getting used to with Nigel, but today made it all worthwhile for her. Today, Victoria saw progress, and that's all she's prayed for.

"Man, I am tired," Nigel said as they walked through the door coming home from the restaurant.

"Me too," Raymond said but looked at Victoria, winking at her, and continued to say, "I guess I'm not too tired."

"Pops, one thing you should know, I am 14 years old, so I already know what that means," Nigel said.

"Then you won't be shocked about the noise you will hear," Raymond said.

"Yo, man, that's grimmy!" Nigel said while at the same time, Victoria yelled, "Raymond!"

"Son, just go to your room and close your door," Raymond said as he continued smiling.

"That's nasty. Y'all wildin' out!" said Nigel.

"I can't believe you," Victoria said.

"You know me, so don't even trip," Raymond said.

Nigel went to his room and turned the television up loud and topped it off by putting on his game console headphones. Ray and Victoria laughed because they knew why he had his television so loud.

"I'm getting ready to go take a nice bubble bath," Victoria said.

"I'm on my way to the kitchen. Do you want anything?" Ray asked.

"Yes, could you bring me up a glass of prune juice, please?"

"Prune juice?"

"Yes, prune juice."

"You *must* not want any of this tonight," Raymond said pointing to his body.

Victoria laughed and said, "Why do you say that?"

"You and prune juice don't mix."

"I'll be alright. You'll see."

Raymond went to the kitchen to get something for him and his wife to drink while relaxing in the bubble bath. Victoria reminisced about the day's affairs. After a long month, she was finally able to exhale. She gave no thought that her sister Niriya would be there in a matter of days. Victoria always takes a bath at night because she never knows when her husband wants to lay with her. She figured her husband wanted to lay next to a wife that smells like a garden, as fresh as a flower. In particular, this night, the pleasant aroma of a sexy, subtle scent to bring to life the very nature of her husband.

Raymond came back upstairs, put both of their drinks on the dresser, put on a little mood music, made sure he was straight and put on some Marksman cologne, which is Victoria's favorite scent for him. He was really doing it big because they hadn't been intimate since his wife told him what she had done.

"You look so beautiful," Raymond said to his dark-skinned wife who was standing in front of him with her naturally curly long hair, big brown eyes, size eight body frame, hips that holds up her bottom frame really lovely, and wearing a sexy teal, spaghetti-strapped, back exposed, very short negligee.

"The beauty doesn't stop at just what you see here."

"What does that mean?"

"You shall feel my beauty as well," Victoria said as she backed up to her 5' foot "10" inches, muscular, low fade haircut, dark-skinned, and part of the beard gang king to their king size bed.

"Uhm…show me all your beauty."

Victoria kissed her husband passionately, and he returned the favor. They filled their lovemaking with not only actions but with words like, "I love you," "I seek to please you," and more. They connected on levels that they hadn't connected on in years. Victoria forgot how good it could feel, and Raymond realized what he'd been missing.

Afterward, Raymond held Victoria in his arms as she laid on his chest. Victoria began to cry softly so she wouldn't wake up Raymond. She was inwardly thanking Me for today. Victoria hadn't felt her husband's love like that because he withheld it from her. He went on day by day after Nigel left as if a part of him had died.

"Are you crying?" Raymond asked, feeling the wetness on his chest.

"No," Victoria replied.

"I know it wasn't that bad…was it?" Raymond asked.

Victoria giggled and said, "No, that's just it. It was wonderful."

He touched her face and said, "Yes, you are. What are the tears for?"

"Do you realize that this is the first time we had made love since the incident a month ago?"

"Yes."

"I thought your love for me was surely lost."

"My love for you was never lost, but it was tested. People fail to realize that love never said that it wouldn't hurt, nor did it say that it didn't need time to heal. When Jesus hung on the cross, He endured pain, suffering, and the loss of His Father's presence…which was more than any of us could imagine. The love I have for you endured somewhat of the same thing. Just as love kept Jesus from leaving the cross, it's the same kind of love that keeps me from leaving you. I love you, Ria."

"I know, and I'm so sorry."

"You don't have to apologize anymore. Stop being down on yourself. You know what I noticed today?"

"What's that?"

"You finally breathed. For the past month, you have been on pins and needles trying to do everything right and trying not to offend."

"I know. I didn't want to cause any more trouble than I already had."

"Let it go now. There is no reason to hold on to it anymore."

"I'm going to try, but it's hard."

"Know that God has forgiven you, and so have I."

"Thank you, sweetheart."

The next morning after their heart-to-heart talk, they were all giggly towards one another. They looked like two high school kids in love. Victoria went downstairs to cook everyone breakfast. This is the first day that Raymond goes back to work. She can't deny that it's going to be awkward to be home alone with Nigel for an entire day. Breakfast is finished and she called them down to eat.

"Everything looks delicious," Raymond said.

"Well, thank you," Victoria said.

"Stop tha cap!" Nigel said.

"What?" asked Raymond.

"Is this how y'all act after doin' the do?" Nigel asked.

They both laughed and Raymond said, "Eat your breakfast, boy."

"I'm just sayin'…it's gross," Nigel said.

"You'll understand someday," Raymond said.

"I've had sex before, and it ain't that big a deal," Nigel said.

Victoria dropped her plate, and Raymond sat there with his mouth opened. Needless to say, that wiped all the smiles off of their faces. "You what," said Victoria.

"What did your mother have to say about this?" Raymond asked.

"She just told me to use protection," Nigel answered.

"But you are only fourteen years old," Victoria said.

"So," Nigel said.

"So? Keep it, respectful son," Raymond said.

"A lot of my friends are smashin'. Man, that's how we do it in Cali," Nigel said.

"I don't know what's wrong with y'all children today. You want to grow up so fast. We do not accept sex before marriage. If I catch you with a young lady in any bedroom before marriage…it's on," Raymond said.

"I hear what you are sayin', but just like a lot of my friends, our fathers weren't around. This is how we were taught to be a man," Nigel said, looking at Victoria.

"Don't look at her. She has paid for what she has done. Victoria, hold your head up," Raymond said as he looked her way after addressing Nigel.

"Why does she get off the hook? It's her fault that you weren't around to teach me what being a man is really about," Nigel said.

"She didn't get off the hook. Either way, it's not only her fault. Your mother was in on it too. I'm not speaking bad or against your her, but she didn't help matters any," Raymond said.

"Don't blame my moms. She did what she had to do," Nigel said.

"It doesn't matter…back to the subject at hand. Do you know why you don't feel the way we do after sex?" Raymond asked.

"Why?" Nigel retorted.

"Because you are not in covenant with that female. I'm in covenant with Victoria because she is my wife. Son, all I can do is lead you from here. I'm sorry I wasn't there for you when you needed me, but I'm here now. You will do what you want to do, but I hope and pray you do what I encourage you to do. All I'm asking is that you wait till you are married," Raymond said.

"I can't make no promises," Nigel said.

"Just consider it," Victoria said.

"Yeah," Nigel answered.

They all finished breakfast. Although he really wanted to stay after that talk at the breakfast table, Raymond headed off to work. Raymond didn't know how things would work with Nigel and Victoria being home by themselves cause all he knew was Nigel didn't care much for his wife. As Raymond was talking to Nigel, Victoria knew she had to talk to Nigel one on one. She felt My unctioning. After she cleaned the kitchen, she called Nigel downstairs.

"Nigel, can you come to the living room, please?" Victoria yelled to the top of the stairs.

He walked down and said, "What's good?"

"Come and let me talk to you for a minute?"

"I really don't want to talk right now."

"Please. This won't take long."

Nigel sat down on the couch with an attitude and said, "What now?"

Victoria took all the disrespect (which reminded her of her sister) and began talking with Nigel. "I want to start off by saying that I'm sorry. I know what I did was wrong, and I can't change that, but I can change our future. I took the first step by confessing what I did."

"But what does that change? Does it change my past? Does it change how cold my mother is and how she treats me because of what you did? Does it change that I didn't have a father growing up? Tell me, what does it change?"

"Nigel, you are absolutely right. It doesn't change your past and all that you went through, but will you allow me to change your future?"

"Ms. Victoria, when I first found out years ago, I didn't like you. When I finally heard from you, I liked you even less."

"Years ago? What are you talking about?"

"My mother told me when I was eleven years old when I asked her about my father."

"What all did she tell you?"

"She told me that you couldn't have babies, so you asked her to have a baby for you and pops. She said you became jealous when you saw that dad didn't care nothing about you but gave his attention to me. She tried to be nice to you, but you wouldn't listen."

"I didn't become jealous, Nigel. Some adult things happened which I'm not at liberty to share with you, but I will tell you this, it wasn't jealousy."

"Y'all weren't in no Jerry Springer type mess, were you? I already feel like some trailer park welfare case."

"Why?"

"Because my aunt is my dad's wife and mom's sister. That's just too much family, and I don't see what's so funny."

"You right; it's not funny. Let me stop laughing. Seriously though, this ain't Jerry Springer. Your mom was artificially insemination. There was no funny business. You were supposed to be ours, but it didn't turn out that way."

"Why not?"

"That's something that your father, mother, and I will all have to sit down with you and talk about. I don't want anything getting whishy-washy or misconstrued."

"When will that be?"

"I don't know. I will talk to your dad about it, alright."

"That's cool."

"Nigel, I also want to let you know that you can't keep holding this over my head. I feel bad enough about it as it is. God has forgiven me, and so has your father. I'm not asking for you to forgive me right away. I know it will take some time."

"Fo sho."

"But what I am asking is that you do not continue to throw it up in my face."

"I can't make promises…but I will try. I'm doing this for my dad, not for you. It wasn't his fault, and I can't punish him for it."

"All I'm asking is that you try, and that will be good enough for me."

"Is that all?"

"Yes. You can go back to doing what you were doing."

Victoria felt a little more confident after the talk with Nigel, and he was still in the same place but could stomach her a little better. It may not seem like much, but it's a start. I'm doing My work, but I do things in My timing, as you all should know. Raymond called every hour to check on his son and wife. Going back to work was a little hard for him. His heart was still at home. There was a lot for Raymond to do, mainly because he left in the middle of a big production. Everyone understood his situation and was lenient with him, but now they needed him to focus and put his hands to the plow.

"Raymond, let me catch you up on what has been going on around here," Joshua said.

"Alright, how far am I backlogged?" Raymond asked.

"Ha, ha, man, do you even want to know?" Joshua said.

"Don't hurt me too bad," was Raymond's response.

"I'll try. But seriously though, here is where we're at with the Dolan Productions. First off, we have a "diva" who thinks she can't be replaced. Fred wants a fifteen-million-dollar movie on a $10,000 budget…so you know how that's going," Joshua said.

"Enough said," Raymond said.

"Man, it's been a madhouse," said Joshua.

"Out of one frying pan to another, huh?" Raymond said.

"What does that mean? What happened at home?"

"It was rough at first. Nigel and Victoria did not get along."

"That's to be expected."

"But things got better as time went on. Nigel still doesn't like Victoria, but he is staying respectful."

"So, what else happened?"

"After referring those two, I was able to spend time with Nigel, and it was great getting to know him all over again. He's smart but very rough around the edges. His mama got him bitter."

"Personally, Raymond, I don't think his mother had to work that hard to make him do that."

"I know, but he's so mad, angry about everything. I have a lot of work to do. Enough about my family. What else is going on around here?"

"I'm not the one to sound like no chick but get this. Have you noticed a change or anyone missing from the office?"

"Not really. I've been preoccupied. What's up?"

"Come to find out, Kareem and Willa had been sleeping together."

"What!?"

"Yes, sur and Willa's husband came up here and wrecked shop. That's why you see all the new stuff. Man, he wiped the floor with Kareem and dragged Willa out by her hair. The cops were here and everything."

"What did Mr. Balstic have to say about all of this?"

"He kicked up his feet and watched the whole thing. Ray, I was on the floor laughing. It was crazy."

"Are you serious? Our "don't play" boss kicked up his feet?"

"Yeah."

"That's crazy and funny at the same time."

Raymond was cracking up at the story. He needed the release to get himself together and his mind back on his work. The fellas talked some more than got back to work. As the day went on, Raymond realized that maybe he'd been gone too long. The workload was a mess. There were tough decisions to make. He had to think about what could go and what needed to stay to meet this impossible budget that the production company put on them. The first order of business is to check out this "diva" that Joshua was talking about. Raymond could have cared less about these uptight, think they're right, stuff don't stink celebrities. He is exceptionally good at his job, and that's why his boss Mr. Balstic entrusted him with this production company.

As Raymond was cleaning up at work, Victoria was cleaning up at her parent's house. Niriya is coming home in a few more days. She's kind of on edge because she hasn't seen her sister in ten years. She sent child support by mail, and that was the extent of their relationship. Victoria knew trouble would brew once Niriya got to town.

Nigel met some boys in the neighborhood, but he's not fitting in because the boys around the neighborhood are rich. They are not his cup of tea. Nigel is rough and "hood," and the other boys can't really handle it except one of them who really wants to be "hood," which is totally out of character for him. Nigel sees it too, and it irritates him, but since Don is the only one that accepts him, Nigel deals with it.

He knows he will have to go to school with these preppy kids. He wants to go to public school. He can't even see himself in a uniform. Nigel has a month before his freshman year of school starts, and he's steadily trying to convince his father to let him go to public school. All his dad is talking about is the private school, but Nigel isn't feeling it at all. He can't wait for his mother to arrive, and he will try to convince her instead.

Anxiously awaiting his mother's arrival for the last few days, Nigel finally gets to see her. Raymond and Victoria are waiting for Niriya's flight to arrive. After a few minutes passed, Nigel saw his mother and went to her.

"Hey, ma," Nigel said as he hugged her.

"Hey boy, don't be gettin' all emotional on me," Niriya said.

"I'm glad you are here. I've missed you," Nigel said.

"Man, being here done made you soft. What they do to you?" Niriya said.

"That ain't funny, ma," Nigel said.

While they were talking catching up, Raymond and Victoria walked up to Niriya and said, "Hello, Niriya."

"Hi Raymond," Niriya said, totally ignoring Victoria and rolling her eyes at her too.

"You don't see my wife standing here. Don't start that foolishness," Raymond said.

"Don't tell me what to do! Just grab my bags so we can go," Niriya said and walked off with Nigel in tow.

Raymond was furious, and Victoria was ticked off, but she kept quiet. One, she didn't want to make a scene. Two, she wanted the reunion with Nigel to be a pleasant one. Raymond thought about getting her luggage, but the way she acted —he could show her better than he could tell her. So, he left her luggage right there at the baggage claim. Victoria was laughing so hard on the inside she had tears coming out of her eyes. As Nigel and his mother walked to the car, Raymond unlocked it so they could get in it. Niriya hadn't even noticed that Raymond didn't have her luggage. Raymond and Victoria sat in the front seat and drove off, then sat quietly in while Nigel and Niriya caught up.

"What have you been doing up here?" Niriya asked.

"Me and dad been hanging out. It's been cool," Nigel said, excluding Victoria.

"What kind of things did y'all do?" Niriya asked.

"Fishing, shopping, playing games, going to the pool hall; stuff like that."

"Poolhall? Uhm."

"What ma?"

"I didn't think underage children are supposed to go to a pool hall."

"It was a'ight. Pops didn't drink or smoke or anything like that. We just played pool and darts, watched some sports, and ate. It's a man thang ma."

"What else did you do?"

"We hooked up the house for you, so you wouldn't have to do a thang once you got there."

"That's the least that could be done."

"How's "Slim"?"

"I dropped him. He got on my nerves."

"Another one bites the dust, huh, ma?"

"You know how I do."

"Yeah, I know how you do."

"What's that supposed to mean?"

"Nothin'."

"Where does everybody want to eat," Raymond asked.

"Let ma choose. It's her ol' stomping ground," Nigel suggested.

"I'm sure thangs have changed over the last ten years since I've been gone," Niriya said.

"Alright. Niriya, what do you want to eat?" Raymond asked ignoring her snide comment.

"Y'all got a burger joint 'round here?" Niriya asked.

"Yeah! Hey Pops, take her to the one you took me to," Nigel said.

"Will do," Raymond said.

"It's in the hood, and it's bangin'," Nigel said.

"Raymond, take me home first," Victoria said.

"Awh, poor little victim can't be 'round folk," Niriya said.

Victoria ignored her comment and said to Raymond, "Just take me home. Y'all can go."

"Don't let her get to you," Raymond said.

"It's okay. I want Nigel to be able to enjoy his mother. I'll be alright," Victoria said.

"You sure?" Raymond asked because he knew where this was going.

"Yeah," Victoria said.

"Ma, you gone like this place," Nigel said.

"Really?" Niriya said.

"Yeah, I bet this gone be your new spot," Nigel said.

"We'll see," Niriya said.

Raymond took Victoria home then drove to the burger joint. He didn't like what Victoria pulled at all. He was upset but didn't want Niriya to see it because he knew she would start some mess, and he was right because as soon as Victoria got out of the car, she hopped in the front seat. Raymond was starting to see what Victoria was talking about all those years ago.

Raymond said, "Get back in the back seat. Nigel, come and sit up here." Nigel said, "I'm good. I don't want to sit up there." Niriya said, "That's my boy," as she snuggled herself in the front seat. Nigel was in the backseat smiling and enjoying all that he was watching. They arrived at the burger joint, and Niriya said, "Ahhh, the smell of grease."

"I told you; wait till you eat the food," Nigel said.

They approached the counter and began to order their food. "Can I have the number four but add bacon and cheddar to the BLT," Nigel ordered.

"What sides do you want with that?" the cashier asked.

"Potato fries and the drink to be a coke," Nigel finished.

"Raymond, what do you suggest that I get?" Niriya asked, trying to make it seem like they were together.

"Nigel, you know what your mother likes. Help her out," Raymond said as he stepped away from her.

"Ma, you gotta get the BLT. Just add bacon to it. I know you don't like cheddar. Get the fries too," Nigel said.

"I'll have what he just said and my drink to be Mountain Dew," Niriya said.

"Hey, Mr. Ray! How are you doing?" the cashier said with a smile.

"Oh, you know Raymond?" Niriya asked.

"Yeah, Mr. Ray and Mrs. Vikki come in here all the time," the cashier said.

"I'm doing good, Sasha. How are you?" Raymond said.

"I'm good," Sasha said.

"This is my son Nigel and his mother Niriya," Raymond said, and Sasha had a look on her face that said, "Surprise!"

"I didn't know you had a son," Sasha said.

"It's a long story, Sasha. Raymond and I will have to tell you all about it one day," Niriya said.

Sasha looked at her and didn't get a good vibe and said, "Oh…okay."

"Never mind what she's talking about, Sasha," Raymond said.

She smiled understanding and said, "Your son is cute, Mr. Ray."

"You don't look too bad yo'self lil ma," Nigel said.

"Alright, you two," Raymond said.

They laughed, and Sasha said, "What can I get for you, Mr. Ray?"

"I'll have what Nigel is having," Raymond said.

"Alright, your order will be out to you in about five minutes," Sasha said.

Raymond paid for the meal, and they went to sit down. He really wished Victoria were there. He didn't mind being there with his son, but Niriya was another story.

"So, what have you been up to, Raymond? We didn't get a chance to talk on the phone long when you guys called," Niriya said.

"I'll be right back. I'm going to the restroom," Nigel said.

Niriya nodded her head, and he left. Then Raymond answered her question, "I've been working a lot and being involved with the ministry."

"Ministry?" Niriya said.

"Yes, ministry."

"Doing what?"

"Teaching and doing whatever the pastor needs help with."

"You must do it by yourself because I know that Ms. High & Mighty couldn't have been up in church with what she has done."

"Let's get something straight right now, Niriya. You are not here to disrupt, disrespect, or disturb my wife. You will leave that crap in Cali. You played a part too. You knew where we lived and my phone number, and you could have made that call, but you chose not to, so don't try to play the victim game. Victoria is my wife and always will be, and there ain't nothing you can do about it. Do you understand me?"

"Let me set you straight. Victoria did this, not me. She paid me to leave. I didn't leave on my own. She jacked up her own life when she made a conscious decision to pull the crap that she did. I don't forgive her, nor will I forget. And as far as me doing something about her being your wife, we'll see."

"Just know this, I will send you away…," Raymond stopped speaking because Nigel walked up.

"What was y'all talking about?" Nigel asked.

"Nothing," Raymond answered.

Sasha brought them their food, and it looked delicious. Nigel slipped her his phone number, and she accepted it with a smile. She walked away and said, "Enjoy."

"Fo' sho,'" Nigel answered.

"Thanks, Sasha," Raymond said.

They ate and had conversation. Raymond let Nigel and his mom do most of the conversing because he had nothing to say. He did not want to talk to Niriya nor give her any inclination that she was on the level. Nigel filled his mother in on what was going on, and then he started the school conversation.

"Ma, Pops, want me to go to this preppy school, but I want to go to public school."

"Raymond, why would you put him in a private school anyway? You know he ain't no uppity kid."

"Niriya, I want the best for him. Just because he started out one way doesn't mean he can't end up better than what he is."

"So, pops, you sayin' I ain't good enough?"

"That's not what I'm saying at all. We all can better ourselves. We don't have to stay the same."

"See Nigel that's that uppity ninja crap. You livin' under my roof and what I say go, and if you want to go to public school, then that's where you will go."

"I'm not going to argue with y'all. If public school is where you want to go, then go ahead, but I'm tellin' you, private school will be way better for you."

"So you say pops."

"It's what I know. You know what, better yet, I'm going to give you one year at public school. If you don't do well or get into any trouble, then I'm going to take you out of that school and put you where I want you to be, and your mother will not have any say so."

"I always got a say-so about my son's education Raymond."

"No, you don't; you just got a say so as long as it causes trouble. This conversation is done."

Raymond left the table to go to the restroom to take a breather leaving Nigel and his mother to talk.

While they were out to eat, Victoria was at home on the phone with her bestie Leigha telling her what happened at the airport.

"And you didn't say anything?" Leigha asked.

"No, I didn't want to start nothing," said Victoria.

"And you didn't; she did."

"I know but I want Nigel to see that I'm not trying to cause anymore trouble."

"I'm sorry, Vikki, but all Nigel is seeing is that his momma is punkin' you. You need to stand up for yourself."

"I will, but it has to be the right time and the right place."

"Right place! Right time! Gurl bye! Couldn't be me."

"Can you understand the position I'm in?"

"Yeah, but I don't see why you have to take so much. You always do this."

"Do what?"

"Never stand up for yourself."

"God vindicates me."

"You need to leave that God crap in the Bible. He didn't tell you to be no punk. I know the scripture."

"What scripture do you know?"

"Eye for an eye and tooth for a tooth."

"But did you finish reading the rest of that scripture? It says, "But I say unto you, That ye resist not evil: but whosoever shall smite thee on thy right cheek, turn to him the other also.""

"I don't know much about scripture, but I'm fairly sure God don't want you not to hit somebody back if they hit you. At least understand the scripture before you blurt it out to fit your situation. Look, Victoria, when one of God's children offends Him, does He not correct them?"

"Yes."

"Then, why shouldn't you?" Victoria didn't have a response, and it grew quiet on the phone. "That's what I thought. Standing up for yourself is not a crime nor a sin. You have the right to do so."

"I'm just trying to be wise about this whole thing. I did bring this on myself."

"You really need to stop that."

"Stop what?"

"That self-pity crap. You already came clean and told Raymond about it. Don't keep beating yourself up over this. Stop punishing yourself. You are doing more harm to you than anything Niriya can do."

"Leigha, you don't know what you're talking about."

"You know I'm right and until you confront her, Niriya is going to keep beating you up. The only way to stop her is to stand up to her."

"I'm going to go now. I'll talk to you later."

"I love you, Vikki; just know that."

"Yeah, I know. Bye."

Victoria was mad and didn't want to admit that what Leigha was saying was right. She got in her car and took a drive out to the pond. She always goes there to think about things. As she sat there on the bench, she began to cry. The more she sat, the more she cried. I stayed silent because she didn't want to hear anything I had to say. Victoria is asking Me many questions in her head, but I refuse to speak because she refuses to listen.

Raymond, Niriya, and Nigel came home while Victoria was out. He took them to their house, and Niriya was ungrateful. She thought it was owed to her. Instead of saying thank you, she walked through the house with her nose in the air and made herself at home. Before Raymond headed home, Niriya forgot her luggage in the trunk of the vehicle and went to catch him before driving off. "Ray! Hold up. Get me my luggage and bring it in," she said. "I don't have your luggage," he said. "What you mean you ain't got my luggage? I told you to put it in the trunk at the airport," she said. "And I sat it right on the curb. So, I don't have your luggage but the airport does cause you ain't gone talk to me like you crazy and think I'm going to do anything for you. Call the airport. I'm sure they'll help you," he said and drove off. Niriya stood there in disbelief. Raymond went back home, saying nothing more to Niriya. When he found out that his wife wasn't there, he called her on the cell phone.

"Hello," she answered.

"Where are you?" he asked.

"I'm out here at the pond."

"What is on your mind?"

"Why you ask me that?"

"Because that's the only time you go there is when you have something on your mind."

"I'm fine, Ray."

"No, you're not. I can tell."

"How did everything go at dinner?"

"It was fine. I wish you were there, though. I really don't think you should have left me alone with her."

"I know, but I couldn't take sitting there with her, and I knew Nigel really wanted to go and eat with you and his mom."

"When are you coming home?"

"I'm on my way now."

"I brought you some food back. I got you your favorite."

"Thank you. See you in a minute."

"I love you, Ria."

"I love you too, Ray."

When she got home, Victoria ate dinner and laid on the couch with Raymond. They sat and watched law dramas on television. She rested in his lap while he slid his fingertips up and down her arm. That always puts her to sleep. He didn't bother her with sex. He could tell that was the last thing on her mind. After the show, he carried her upstairs and put her in bed. She didn't ask about Niriya or Nigel nor about her sister's negative thoughts concerning the house. Victoria could have cared less.

Back at Niriya's, Nigel settled in bed, and she stayed up enjoying being in the house she grew up in but hated it at the same time because of all the heartache she went through. On her first night in her "new" home, Niriya had a flashback when her parents kicked her out of the house. "I'm sick of this, Niriya. I've done all I can for you, but all you care about is bringing these different boys into MY house and laying around! I'm tired! I'm tired of this! I'm tired of you!" said Niriya's mom.

"Oh, you tired of me! I don't need this, and I don't need you!" said Niriya.

"Niriya, we've been more than fair to you. We've given you all kinds of breaks, and we ask very little of you, and all you've done is spit in our faces. What else do you expect for us to do?" Niriya's dad said.

"I don't expect anything from you," Niriya cried.

"What happened to you, Niriya? We didn't raise you like this," her mom said.

"Don't worry about it! You don't care! All you care about and ever cared about is your high society status and how Victoria fit that status and how I never did. You never loved me like you did her. I'm tired of being in her shadow," Niriya yelled.

"That's not true, and you know it. If I did for one, I did for the other, always," her mom said.

"I'm not talking about things. I'm talking about love. Why can't you love me, momma?" Niriya said breaking down sobbing.

"I do love you, Niriya, but you make it hard. What about the chances your father and I gave you? That wasn't love? What about going to court for you time after time? That wasn't love? I don't want to hear about you not being loved. I loved until it hurt. But now, it's time for you to leave," her mom said as she turned her back.

"Pamela, no; don't do this," Niriya's father said.

"Dad, it's okay. I'll leave, but before I go, momma, I want you to know all I ever cared about was loving and pleasing you. I tried, but you never saw past my mistakes to see the good I did and the tries I tried. I love you anyway, momma," Niriya said as she left the house. Her father, Donnie, just looked at his wife in disgust. Things didn't get better for a long time after that. All he saw was the pain in his daughter's eyes.

Niriya sat on the couch in tears and said, "Momma, why?"

"Ma, you a'ight?" Nigel asked as he walked into the living room to snap her out of the memory.

She wiped her tears and said, "I'm fine, just glad to be home."

"Even if your sister is here," Nigel asked, wondering if she really felt something for Victoria.

"I could do without her, but it's been years since I've been back here, and it's just great to be back," Niriya said.

"Do you really hate her like that?" Nigel asked.

"She has been a thorn in my side since we were kids."

"I'mma leave that alone. It's time for you to go to bed ma. Come on."

Niriya followed her son upstairs and laid on her new king-size bed. There wasn't a difference for Nigel since his room at his own house was just as nice as the one at his father's. Everyone's back in Jacksonville, and Niriya is ready to make waves. Now the real fun begins.

The More Things Change

The next morning, Raymond left for work, and Victoria left to get away from Niriya. She knew that would be double trouble. Both Nigel and Niriya…that's a fight waiting to happen. Raymond couldn't call as much as Victoria wished because he was so busy playing catch up. He could even foresee late nights.

Victoria asked Leigha to come to brunch with her. Joshua walked up and said, "Hey Victoria, " As they sat there talking. How are you doing?"

"Hi, Joshua. I'm well. How about yourself?" Victoria asked.

"Doing good, just getting something to eat early because I'm not going to be able to take a lunch today," Joshua said.

"Why?" Victoria inquired.

"I have some appointments about the production this afternoon," Joshua replied.

"Oh, okay," Victoria said.

"Who is this lovely young lady?" Joshua asked, eyeballing her best friend.

"My bad. I guess that was rude of me. But wait, you don't remember her?"

"Uh, I'm sorry. I don't," Joshua said.

"From our wedding? I mean you guys walked down the aisle together," Victoria said.

"That was almost 20 years ago, Victoria," Joshua said.

"I guess so. Well, anyway, Joshua, this is my best friend Leigha, and Leigha, this is Raymond's best friend Joshua," Victoria introduced.

"Hello," Leigha said as she shook the hand Joshua extended.

"Nice to meet you again," he said with a sly grin.

"Same here," Leigha said returning the flirtatious favor.

"So, how is that sexy husband of mine?" Victoria interrupted.

"He's good, just extremely busy with the production. But Raymond has been in a really good mood lately. I haven't seen him this happy in a while," he said.

"Yes, I know," Victoria replied.

"No offense," Joshua said.

"None taken," Victoria replied.

"Well, I gotta go," Joshua said.

"Alright, tell my husband I said I love him," Victoria said.

"Will do, and Leigha, I hope to see you around soon," Joshua said with a nod leaving the table.

"You don't have to wait," Leigha said with a sly grin. Victoria kicked her leg up under the table, and Leigha screamed, "Ouch! What?" Victoria gave her a nod as if to say, "straighten up."

"I'm going to the restroom. I'll be back," Leigha said.

As Victoria sat at the table waiting for Leigha's return, she must have had an intense look on her face because there was a man who was watching her from across the room. "Excuse me, miss, but are you alright?" this strange man asked as he walked up to her table.

"Yes, thank you," Victoria said.

"I'm sorry, but I just don't believe that," the strange man said and sat down.

"Excuse me, but what do you think you are doing?"

"I just came to make you smile. You look like you need someone to talk to."

"I'm fine. I have a husband and a best friend to talk to if need be."

"Let me introduce myself. My name is Tracey."

"Hi, Tracey. You'd have to pardon me if I don't tell you my name."

"It's alright. I understand. You don't know me from a hole in the wall."

"Exactly."

"I only wanted to encourage you and say that it's going to be alright. God has everything under control, but there's something you must do."

"Yeah, and what is that?"

"You are going to have to stand up for yourself and stop running from your problems. Even now, you are here because you are running from someone. This is not your normal routine."

Victoria's eyes became huge. She was shocked at what this man said to her…reading her like a book. "Oh wow, how did….."

"I only speak what the Father gives me to speak. Have a blessed day Victoria," Tracey said as he got up from the table to leave.

"Bu..bu..but."

"How did I know?"

"Yes."

"Like I said, I only speak what the Father tells me too. Enjoy the rest of your day." Tracey left while Leigha walked up and said to Victoria, "Who was that?" in excitement.

"Some man named Tracey," Victoria answered.

"My God! One thing I can say about your God is that He has blessed my day because there is no lack of sexy men ta-day," Leigha said.

"Girl, you are so crazy," Victoria said laughing.

"Sooo, what-did-he-want?" Leigha asked being nosey.

"Nothing," Victoria said.

"He was sitting at the table, talking to you quite comfortably. He didn't want just nothing," Leigha said.

"What about you?"

"What do you mean?"

"That sure was a long restroom break."

"Yeah, and?"

"And…what took you so long?"

"Dawggone, do I have to tell you when I wipe my butt cheeks too?"

"You know what, don't make me bust you out. I am not slow chick."

"I don't know what you are talking about." They both laughed, and Leigha asked, "What's up with brotha man?"

"I told you, nothing. I don't even know the guy."

"No, not him, Joshua?"

"He's cool. We all grew up together. Ray and Joshua been tight since their momma's pushed them out the womb. But we didn't meet them until we were in middle school when we moved into the neighborhood."

"I'm surprised we've never met before now. I mean outside of the wedding."

"Yeah, probably because of where we all lived and went to school. Those school zones were crazy. You and I went to school together, and they went to school together, but we all lived in the same neighborhood."

"Y'all did, but I was across the way in the hood."

"Chile, we had so much fun in the hood though."

"Right! I was surprised your mother allowed you to hang out with me, especially where I lived."

"Oh, trust me she tried to make it hard. But she knew where she came from, no matter how hard she tried to forget."

"Bump all that. What's up with ya boi?"

"Joshua?"

"Don't play dumb. What is his software?"

"What!"

"You knooooww…his program. Is his software compatible with my computer?"

"I don't know that! I have not slept with him. What kind of woman do you think I am?"

"No, I'm not talking about sex. I'm talking about his 4-1-1."

"Oh, you know I never know what you be talking about."

"Duh! So, what is it?"

"He's single."

"Check, download program."

"He works side by side with my husband."

"A job too! Check, install accepted."

"He goes to church."

"Eh, I can deal with that notification. I guess, just as long as he goes to church."

"No, honey, that man is saved."

"Whelp, that killed that vision; uninstall software."

"Girl, what is wrong with you? What vision?" Victoria said laughing.

"While y'all were talking, I was thinkin' bout some thangs."

"I don't know what I'm going to do with you. That's why I kicked you because you were addressing a man of God."

"You should have told me when I got up to go to the restroom."

"Why do you say that?"

"Because I wouldn't have taken his number," Leigha said as she threw his number in the trash as they got up to leave the restaurant.

"Wow! You are a piece of work," Victoria said.

"Well, Vic, I gotta get to work. I will holla at you later," Leigha said.

"Alright, then. Thanks for coming to brunch with me," Victoria said.

"Anytime," Leigha said as they parted ways.

Victoria went to her car quietly. She couldn't say anything because she was still in awe about what had just happened. I had to get to her somehow because she wasn't receiving what her husband, nor what her best friend was saying. It's crazy how I have to send a perfect stranger to get a message to My people because they won't listen to the ones that love them that I speak through. Why so hard-headed? (Smh) I don't know about My children sometimes.

Victoria didn't know what to do with the rest of her day. She knew she'd better heed what I instructed, but she didn't know how to apply what I spoke to her. I know what's in her heart, but I'm waiting for her to admit to it first.

After brunch, she called her husband at work. "Hey, cutie," Raymond answered the phone.

"Hey love, how are you doing?" Victoria asked.

"Busy. There is a lot here I have to do. I didn't know it would be like this from me taking a vacation. I've hardly taken any vacation. It's never been like this before," Raymond said.

"Is it going to be a late-night?"

"Looks that way. What do you have planned today?"

"I don't know. It's all kind of up in the air."

"Do you want to have lunch together?"

"Are you sure you're going to have the time?"

"I always have time for my wife."

"Where do you want to go and what time?"

"Just meet me here, and I will take you somewhere special."

"You sure you don't want me to just meet you at the restaurant? You know how traffic is downtown this time of day."

"No, just meet me here."

"Alright, I'll see you at what…12:00?"

"Yes, twelve is good."

"Alright, Ray, I'll let you go."

"See you for lunch."

"I love you."

"I love you too, Ria."

Victoria didn't want to tell Raymond that she'd just eaten brunch. Twelve o'clock was just around the corner, and she was full. However, she had an hour to kill before meeting him. While Raymond waited for his wife to come to his job, he watched the production he had been working on since returning to work. He wanted to see what Joshua was talking about, and it was as he said. The main actress was acting like she couldn't be replaced. So, Raymond had to speak, "Ms. Carrie, can I talk to you for a minute?"

"Sure, Raymond. How can I help you?" the celebrity "diva," Carrie McDonald said.

"Hey Carrie, it's not working out. We are going to have to let you go."

"What! Uh, what do you mean? I'm the best one you have on the set."

"That's the problem right there; you don't think you can be replaced. Everyone on this set is important, and they are good too; otherwise, they wouldn't have the part."

"This movie won't be nothin' without me! You need me! Even if you begged, I wouldn't come back to this worthless movie!"

"Thank you for your time, Carrie. Everything is going to work out fine with or without you. You don't make this movie, everybody does, and that's what you fail to realize."

"Uhm! You will regret this!" Carrie "the star" McDonald said as she "exited the stage."

"Have a wonderful day," Raymond said sarcastically.

After Raymond's victory, it was time for his lunch date with his wife. She was right on time. He watched his beautiful wife walk towards him in her turquoise and cream sundress with her natural, fresh, and full twist out, flawless make-up, summertime jewelry, and turquoise stilettos. He could hardly move, and the men in his office were staring too. Victoria smiled as she walked towards him.

"Wow! You look so beautiful."

"Thank you. You're looking debonair yourself."

"Only for you, babe."

"Ray, man, your wife is *hot*!" one of the new men in the office said.

"Watch yo'self," Raymond said. That slang comes out of him from time to time when he gets mad.

"Aye, man, I'm just sayin'…," the man said.

"Come on, Raymond," Victoria said as she mingled her arm with his.

Raymond looked at his colleague with eyes that sneered. He took Victoria to a classy, upscale restaurant for lunch. They sat outside with the sand and oceanfront view. The seafood was incredible, but Victoria could hardly eat because she was still full from her brunch with Leigha. Victoria didn't want to tell him about her brunch because she knew it would lead to the very reason of why she was there. As they ate, enjoying the view, Raymond asked the unthinkable.

"Have you talked to Niriya and Nigel this morning?"

"No, Raymond. I have not."

"Why are you being short with me? I'm just asking a question."

"I know; I'm sorry. I just don't want to talk about them right now."

"But Nigel is my son, and I can talk about him at any time."

"Yes, but Niriya's another story. And on top of that, we don't need to talk about them every time we're together. This lunch is supposed to be about us."

"True. But you are going to have to face her one day. You can't run from her forever."

"Can we talk about this another time? I want to enjoy lunch with you."

"Sure, but you know we are going to have to talk about it one day."

"Yes, I know."

"Have I told you that you look beautiful today?"

"Yes. Have I told you that I want to take you home?"

"Is that right?"

"Uhm, hmm."

"That's what's up, but I gotta eat first."

"You are so crazy."

Raymond took another bite of his food, wiped his mouth with a napkin, and said to Victoria, "I had to fire someone today."

"Who?"

"Carrie McDonald."

"Carrie McDonald! The famous Carrie McDonald?"

"Yep, that one."

"She's a great actress! I didn't know you were working with her. Why did you fire her?"

"Carrie is great on-screen but a monster behind the film."

"Wow! Really?"

"She thinks the world revolves around her and was making everyone around her miserable. You know what she said when I fired her?"

"What?"

Raymond mocked what Carrie said, sounding and acting just like her. "She said, "This movie won't be nothin' without me! You need me! Even if you begged, I wouldn't come back to this worthless movie!" I just told her thank you and went on about my way."

"That's disappointing. I really liked her, but she seems full of herself."

"If "they say to never meet your heroes" was a person, she'd be it. Her attitude made the whole production intolerable. She was an obstacle that had to be removed so the production can run more smoothly. She had to go."

"I guess you have to do what you have to do. Do you have anyone else in mind to take her spot?"

"We're working on it."

"Who is it?"

"I can't tell you yet."

"Awh, come on; you know I'm not going to say anything."

"I know you're not because I'm not telling you."

"That's messed up. Do you then."

"Always do. That's why I'm good at what I do."

"Whatever."

"Let me ask you a question."

"Man, what do you want to ask me now?"

"You lucky you're beautiful."

"Or what?"

"Oh, I see what you're doing."

"What's that?"

"You want me to put you in your place, but it ain't going to work."

"What you mean?" Victoria said while placing her foot in between his legs.

"Uh, uh, nope. I'm going to ask you the question," he said moving her foot.

"Awh, man! You trippin'. Why are you acting like this?"

"Answer my question, and I'll scratch your itch."

"Go ahead and ask this question that's so important that's causing you to interrupt my dirty thoughts."

"What are you going to do?" Raymond asked.

"What do you mean?" Victoria asked.

"When are you going to do what God has called you to do?"

"I don't know what you are talking about."

"Yes, you do."

"No, I don't."

"I want an answer. I've waited a long time. And been patient."

"I like being home and being there for you. I'm free to do what I want."

"But what about what God wants you to do."

"You know, you're looking good right now."

Trying to be serious, Raymond said with a tight lip, "Don't even try to distract me. Again, get your twinkle toes from between my legs and quit biting your bottom lip and looking at me with those sexy eyes."

Victoria took a piece of ice from her glass of water, slightly glided it across her lips, then dropped it down the top part of her dress seductively. The ice was cold and woke up "the girls." Captivating Raymond's eyes, Victoria said, "You ready?"

Raymond tried to stay focused, but he couldn't wait another second. He saw the waitress and said, "Check, please!"

Victoria gently smiled and said, "I don't know why you tried to resist anyway."

Raymond and Victoria went to a hotel around the corner and did what husbands and wives are meant to do, and they enjoyed every minute of tearing each other's clothes off and giving in to each other's desires. Victoria avoided what was being asked of her, but she will have to answer the question very soon.

Victoria is doing what many of My children do, avoiding My plan for their life. My people fail to realize they eventually have to answer Me. I don't deal in "quid pro quo," this for that. You can't trade off what you want versus My plan for your life. Answer the call! If not, you are doing nothing but holding up your own blessed path. It's not about a blessing. It's about a blessed path. The more you choose to stay on your own path, the more things you will have to deal with that were never designed for you, which will eventually cause you frustration and disappointment. You think it's Me and that I caused it when it's really your path that you're on versus the path I created you to walk. Just like I will give her and Raymond their son in My time, so will I give you what I promised you. But to receive it, you have to be in The Way. Victoria doesn't even realize she's holding up her blessing by not doing what I have asked her to do. Her promise is not predicated upon if I hold up My end of the bargain. I will honor what I said what I was going to do; however, she has a responsibility to Me, and so do YOU. She really doesn't know how happy she could be, and neither do you.

After making love, Raymond returned to work, and Victoria went home. He was refreshed and tired at the same time. It took him a minute to focus on work, but he finally did, as much as he could.

As soon as Victoria hit the house, Niriya was right behind her, walking straight in, and Victoria said, "Excuse me, but this isn't your house, so you are not welcome to walk in!"

"Oh, I gotta knock now?"

"You should be able to answer that for yourself."

"I guess Nigel has to knock too?"

"The answer to that question is that this is his house also. Keywords — his house."

"What is his is mine, and mine is his."

"That may be but only in your house, not mine."

"Hmm…sounds like my sister is getting a backbone."

"Look, I don't have time for your nonsense. Is there something you want?"

"I just wanted to talk to my big sis, see how things are going."

"I'm doing freaking fantastic."

"You are not going to ask how I've been?"

"I don't really care. Now, leave MY house?"

"Do I have any nieces or nephews yet?"

"Oh, you trying to come for me?! It's really time for you to go!"

"Yeah, I'll leave, but you best believe I will be back."

Niriya walked off in a type of way to let you know she's got something under her sleeve. All Victoria could do was ignore her sister, get her shower, take a nap, and later fix dinner for her husband when he gets home from work. Nigel and Niriya walked around the old neighborhood, and he introduced his mom to his new friends. After his escapade with his wife, Raymond couldn't stay on task, so he only worked his regular hours and went home. Victoria was surprised to see him so early.

"What are you doing here?" Victoria asked.

"Is that how you act after our hot rendezvous?" Raymond asked.

"No, I'm just shocked to see you home so early."

"I couldn't concentrate after our "lunch date," so I came home."

"Well, are you ready to eat?"

"You know I'm hungry."

"Boy, you are so crazy."

"Can I show you how crazy I am?"

"Sure, you can," Victoria said.

Raymond took his wife right there in the living room. He loves his wife which is frustrating for him and it confuses him sometimes because any other man would have left her for the type of things she's done. He doesn't understand fully why he stays when everything in him wants to go. Yet, Victoria didn't trust in his love because his love had been on and off for the past ten years. Their marriage was struggling, and she knew it. They would have these escapades, but they wouldn't last long. She just went along for the ride for as long as it would go until it was time to get off. She wondered if his love was genuine or was it only because his son was back. If she had just trusted in Me, she wouldn't be going through what she's going through right now.

Ladies, let Me talk to you for a minute. You cause yourself a lot of pain and trouble, and it's all because you don't trust Me. Your marriages are a mess because you don't trust Me. Single ladies, you can't continue in a relationship because you don't trust Me. You'd rather trust in a meme that connects with your emotions, link up with people who are enduring the same situations, and the hurt you're dealing with, and all y'all are walking into walls. What would you say if I told you that you have already been in the relationship with the man I had for you, but because of your lack of trust in Me, it didn't last or work out? You know for yourself that you missed the mark. It's a hard pill to swallow when you realize you messed up your own blessing. You don't seem to trust the love I've placed in your husband. Whether they are saved or not, you are still his rib. You wonder why you are going through but refuse to look at yourself. You would like to blame "him"; however, it's not all him. Save yourself some trouble; take some time to examine yourself, and you will see that it has nothing to do with "his" love but yours.

Guess what happened next. There was a knock at the door during Raymond and Victoria's "special" moment. Neither one answered the door and continued doing what they were doing, but the knocking persisted. Victoria wrapped herself up in the blanket that hung over the couch and went to the door to see who it was. When she looked out the peephole, she looked over at Raymond and whispered, "It's Niriya." Her sister kept knocking at the door, so Victoria moaned, "Ohhhh, Ray! Oh, Raymond! Yes! Yes! Yes!"

Raymond whispered back with a laugh saying, "You wrong for that, but good looking out. Now come back over here."

Niriya got mad and left. They laughed and went back to "knowing" each other. Victoria felt so good when she did that. She climbed on top of Raymond with confidence and courage. In her own way, she let Niriya feel how she's felt for years but little did she know that just ticked off Niriya, and Victoria wasn't prepared for what she would do next. Niriya went home and got Nigel's key to Victoria's house.

Even though Victoria and Raymond wanted to be left alone to finish what they were doing, Niriya used the key, turned it, and walked straight into her sister's house as if she owned it.

"What is your problem, Niriya!" Victoria yelled as she jumped up and covered herself and her husband.

"Get out of my house!" Raymond yelled.

"Y'all should have answered when I knocked on the door, but no, Ms. Victoria wanted to be funny. I just wanted to show that I got a couple of jokes too," Niriya said with a smile on her face.

"If you trespass again, I will have you locked up," Victoria said.

"And what would Nigel say? Isn't he the important one in this factor?" Niriya said while she stared at Raymond up and down, hoping to get a glance.

"Don't put Nigel in this!" Raymond said while making sure he was wrapped tight.

"No, Raymond, she's right. We don't want Nigel to get hurt," Victoria said.

"Ain't no way, Victoria! She can't do want she wanna do because of Nigel. When are you going to handle your business?" Raymond said.

"We will talk about this later, Raymond. Niriya, get out and give Nigel's key back to him," Victoria said.

"That's right, Ms. High Society, bow down," Niriya said.

"Excuse me?" Victoria said.

"You heard me," Niriya said.

"You a silly trick," Victoria said.

"Yeah, well, this trick just gave you a treat," Niriya said as she slowly closed the door, smiling and winking at Raymond. She listened at the door as they argued.

"Man, that girl know she can jack up a good time. Talk about wanting to go back to work," Raymond said.

"Oh, you ain't going back to work," Victoria said.

"Why not? At least at work, I can trust everybody to hold their own," Raymond said.

"What's that supposed to mean?"

"Just what I said."

"No, tell me, Ray."

"I'm just saying, you need to hold it down. Forget the fact she's your sister; you just let another woman come up in YOUR house and run your home. How do you think that makes me look at you?"

"How do you look at me, Raymond? Please tell me, how do you see me?"

"I don't see a real woman. I can tell you that!"

"That don't shock me. I've never really meant anything to you. Maybe I don't stand up to her because you ain't worth standing up for."

He walked up on her and said, "Oh, is that right?"

She stared back at him in his eyes and said, "Ab-so-freakin-lutely!"

He walked off, headed upstairs, and Victoria yelled, "You don't think I know what I'm doing?"

"Honestly, no…no, I don't, and right now, I don't even give a …. He took a deep breath and said, "Remember, I'm not worth it."

"Well, I do, and you watch and see how it's going to turn out."

"That's what your mouth say. Man, I'm going to bed. You are lucky if I'm here in the morning. Glad I got my nutt off earlier today."

"Oh, no, you didn't! You want me to hold my own? Well, that day has come! Don't you ever in your life disrespect me like that cause next time, you will choke on yo' nutt instead of gettin' it off."

"I wouldn't even waste the next nutt on you. Can't have no mistakes."

Victoria was taken back at what Raymond implied, and with tears in her eyes, she said, "Then don't waste your time walking upstairs to sleep in our bed. Sleep on the couch!"

"Hell naw…this my house! I sleep where I want."

"Is that right?"

"Hell to tha yeah."

"Well then, I can sleep where I want."

"Do you then."

Raymond went upstairs and slammed the door. Victoria put back on her clothes to leave the house. She left to go to Leigha's, and Raymond could cared less. He hated to see his wife act like such a punk, and what she said hurt him to his core. He thought she was stronger than that, which turned him completely off. He believes there is nothing worse than a woman who won't handle her business.

I had to check Raymond, though. He doesn't realize that he's the one that started the fire. Victoria was wrong for what she allowed, but he was wrong for telling her that he did not see her as a real woman. Her response was to what he said to her. It wasn't only her words that cut him to his core, but it was his words that hurt her too. Once he lit that match about her not being a real woman, the argument had no choice but to turn up.

Niriya watched as Victoria pulled out of the driveway, and she quite enjoyed the effect she had on them. Niriya has plans of her own for working this, and she was going to do everything possible to bring her plans to pass. She didn't wait too long after Victoria left to start her plan.

She called Raymond, and he answered the phone, asking, "What do you want?"

"You need someone who is a woman about hers," Niriya said.

"Yeah, I do, but it ain't you," Raymond said.

"It could be," said Niriya.

"I ain't got time for this. Don't call here no more," Raymond said.

"What about Nigel?" Niriya asked.

"Nigel will be taken care of, so don't worry about that. As for you, keep to yourself and leave me the hell alone," Raymond said as he hung up the phone.

Niriya was infuriated. She couldn't believe her plan wasn't working, but she wasn't going to stop. In the meantime, Victoria was in tears and showed up at Leigha's door unannounced.

"What are you doing here?" Leigha asked.

"I really need to talk to you," Victoria said.

"It's really not a good time," Leigha said.

"Come on, please," Victoria begged.

"Alright, come on in," Leigha said.

Victoria walked in and saw a young handsome white man sitting on the couch. She noticed that she may have interrupted an intimate moment. "Oh, I'm sorry. I'll go," said Victoria.

The young man stood up and saw the desperation on this woman's face whom he did not know and said, "Lee, she looks like she really needs you. Call me later or tomorrow."

"Thank you. I will call you tomorrow. She can keep me up for a long time," Leigha said with a smile. Victoria couldn't even muster up a giggle.

"Alright, then. You will make up for this," Matt whispered in Leigha's ear, kissed her on the cheek, and walked out of the house.

"So, what are you in tears for?" Leigha asked a bit irritated. Victoria paused. "Let me guess, Niriya?" Leigha said.

"You know what, I don't need this. I thought I could come to you," Victoria said, heading out the door.

"At least then I could get my groove on," Leigha said.

"Oh, so that's what's important?" Victoria said.

"Get back in here. You know you ain't going nowhere."

"No, get back to your "twat" cause that's what you're thinking with anyway."

"Vikki, I'm sorry. You right…what is going on?"

As Victoria walked sluggishly towards the couch, she said, "How about Raymond and I was in the living room doing our thing, and Niriya walks into the house."

"Noooo, she didn't."

"Yes, she did."

"Did you punch her back out of your house?"

"No, but we jumped up and told her to get out."

"What did Raymond have to say?"

"He was…no, he is still furious."

"I bet."

"Niriya took Nigel's key and used it. We got into it, but I backed down because I don't want Nigel to get hurt."

"Victoria, seriously, when are you going to let go of that crutch?"

"It's not a crutch! Why does everyone keep saying that?"

"If everyone is saying it, then there must be some truth to it."

"Nigel already doesn't like me, and to get into it with his mother will make it even worse. We are not in the same place as when he first came here. I mean, nothing is perfect, but we did finally make a connection...at least to where the sight of me doesn't make him sick."

"Gurl, Nigel will be alright. Remember who his mama is…I'm quite sure he is used to drama and chaos…."

"Yeah, but I don't want to add to it."

"You need to confront and quit playin'. Bump tha dumb ish. Do you want me to get wit' her? You know I will do it."

"No, how does that help?"

"It'll help me, that's for sure."

"All you would do is catch a case."

"Vikki, I don't mind catching a case and you know that. I haven't been in a good fight in a while, and I think it's about that time I brush up on my skills. What you think?"

"I think you have lost your mind. Leigha, you are a grown woman and should be past that fighting stage."

"Please, right about now, you need to get that mentality."

"I need sound help right now, not that foolishness."

"Then you came to the wrong place for that because there is nothing about me that says "sound.""

"Hmmm…you may be right about that."

"I know I'm right. Maybe you should have called your pastor for that, which makes me believe that you want to hear what I have to say because you know the kind of advice I'm going to give you."

"That's crazy. I don't even know why I talk to you."

"Uh, huh, it all makes sense. You have known me since middle school, and you know how I handle problems, plus you know what I'm going to say."

"Trust me, that is nowhere near right."

"Uhm, hmm."

"Anyway, after she left, Raymond and I got into this huge argument."

"About what?"

"He says that I didn't handle my business."

"And you didn't?"

"How can you say that?"

"Victoria, you keep letting Niriya say and do whatever she wants. That would get old real quick."

"I can't worry about what he thinks. I have to wait for the right time."

"What right time? Tonight, was the right time. A few days ago, was the right time. I'm just sayin', ten years ago was the right time. What are you scared of?"

I'm not scared of anything. Look, I'm too tired to talk about this. May I sleep in the guestroom?"

"Sure, but you're still going to have to deal with it tomorrow."

"That's fine. And I didn't mean to interrupt your evening. I'm sorry."

"I was tryin' to get hooked up, but it's cool," Leigha said as they both laughed.

Victoria went upstairs to sleep, and Raymond was at home, pretending as if he didn't care where his wife was laying her head. He'd go crazy if she laid up with another guy. He was confident she'd never do that because that's not the type of person she is. He tossed and turned all night long. He felt bad about what he said to his wife and grasped the concept that maybe she said what she said because of what he said.

Raymond knew he was wrong. Then finally, at three o'clock in the morning, he woke up and called Victoria. He tried and tried, but she didn't answer her phone. She saw him calling but sent him to voicemail every time. He got up, put on his clothes, and searched for her. His first stop was their favorite hotel, but he found out she wasn't there. Then he left for Leigha's house. Raymond rang the doorbell over and over and over again until Leigha answered the door. "What in tha hell is going on tonight! Last time I checked, I wasn't running a brothel. Who is it!" Leigha answered the knock at the door.

"It's Raymond," he answered.

"Raymond, it's almost four in the morning. What do you want?" Leigha asked, half-sleep.

"I'm sorry to disturb you so late but is my wife here?" Raymond asked.

"You know she is," Leigha said, letting him in the house.

"Is she in the guest bedroom?" Raymond asked.

"Yeah," Leigha said.

"You mind if I go up there?" Raymond asked.

"Yeah, but don't start no stuff, Raymond. Ya girl was jacked up when she came over here. Although I agree with you, don't put her through nothing else tonight," Leigha said.

"I got you. I'm not here to hurt her, but you hurtin' me with that breath," Raymond said.

She pushed him and said, "Whateva. Shut up."

Raymond went to the guest bedroom, took off his shoes, and laid next to his wife. Victoria didn't realize he came into the room. Raymond didn't wake her up. It just felt good to him that he was beside her. Victoria felt someone on her after a few minutes. She stayed calm because she smelled the scent of her husband. She turned her head towards him to see him sleep. Then she turned back over to go back to sleep.

The next morning Raymond got up and left to go to work without waking up Victoria. He overslept, so he left in a hurry. Niriya saw Raymond when he got home. He had to stop there first to take care of his personal hygiene. Meanwhile, Victoria got up to go home. And at the same time Victoria was coming home, Niriya took Nigel's key and let herself into Raymond and Victoria's house again. She heard the shower running. She got undressed, leaving on nothing but a purple bra and panty set with her size four coke-bottle figure, flung her long sew-in off her shoulders, and sat on the edge of the bed waiting for Raymond to come out of the shower as she glided her long acrylic fingernails back and forth across the bed. Victoria made it to the house. As she entered her home, Raymond came out of the shower in nothing but a towel wrapped around his waist. All she focused on was this dark-skinned man with the build of Morris Chestnut, bedroom eyes, and with waves so tight in his hair that it would even make a navy captain seasick. Niriya stood up in front of him, smiling, blocking his bathroom doorway, and said, "Mmmm…what I could do with that," as she started to unwrap his towel. Right, when he grabbed her hand, Victoria came into the room simultaneously. Raymond looked at Victoria and Niriya quickly. He knew this didn't look good.

"What in the…! You know what, that is it!" Victoria said.

"Ria baby, it's not what it looks like. I promise you. I didn't even know she was here," Raymond said.

"Why are you lying?" Niriya yelled.

"Shut up!" Raymond said.

"Niriya! Get out of my house now before I mop the floor with you," Victoria yelled.

"You ain't gone do nothing. You've always been weak and ain't nothin' changed about you but your age," Niriya said.

"Ray, I want to see you in the bathroom now!" Victoria said.

"I enjoyed this morning with you, Raymond," Niriya said.

Then, Victoria walked over and punched Niriya in the face, knocking her down to the floor. They tore that bedroom up. Victoria dragged Niriya downstairs by her hair and literally threw her out the door in her bra and panties. Raymond never saw his wife fight before. He didn't know she had hands. It made him kind of proud. Afterward, Victoria went upstairs to handle Raymond.

"What do you think you are doing?" she asked him.

"You can't believe her, Victoria. You can't be serious."

"Dead serious."

"Come on, I just got home. I was with you last night at Leigha's. I came home to get myself ready for work because, as you see, I'm running late. I got into the shower and when I came out is when I saw you and her. I had no clue she was in the house."

"Raymond, how stupid do you think I am? How can you not hear someone coming into the house, let alone walking in the bedroom?"

"I don't know what else to say because it's not how it looked. I didn't do nothing with that girl. Do you think I would have come for you in the middle of the night if I could have gone down the street and slept with her? Come on now."

"Why did you leave without waking me up?"

"Like I said, I was running late. I was going to call you on my way to work. I just wanted to be close to you last night. I know I was wrong in what I said. I couldn't even sleep when you left. Look, Ria, I – don't – want – her!"

"Raymond, I have got to go and get my head together. Too much is going on right now, and it's too much to deal with. I thought things were getting better, but I can't live like this."

"Live like what?"

"This…on pins and needles…all this drama. Everything that has been going on isn't me, and I need to clear my head. I know I did wrong, but I don't deserve this. I shouldn't have said what I said yesterday, either. You are worth it, but I just can't right now. I don't deserve…all this."

"You're right; you don't. Please stay, don't go."

"I have to clear my head, Raymond."

"You need to know I don't want you to leave. You can't run from your problems. That's why you have all this drama because you won't face them. You really need to stay home and handle it."

"I understand that you disagree, but it ain't left up to you. You make threats about leaving all the time, and the moment I make good on *your* threats I need to face my problems."

"I know and I shouldn't make threats about leaving all the time but given everything that has happened, I should have left but didn't. I stay because I face my issues head-on."

"Yeah, well, this time it ain't left up to you."

"It is left up to me. I am the head of this house, and if I say for you not to go, you can't go."

"Who do you think you are?"

"Your husband."

"Whatever! Why are we pretending?"

"Pretending? What…wait a minute…what are you talking about?"

"Our marriage has been on the rocks for the past ten years. I know you see it too."

"No, that has been your guilt. Don't try to put that on me. I love you, always have and always will."

"You can put this all on me, but you bear some weight yourself."

"How so?"

"Your love for me has been off and on since Nigel left."

"You mean forced out."

"I thought you forgave me."

"Why do you think it should be that easy just because you apologized? You can't expect me to be skipping along the sidewalk with my head in the clouds. It is hard. I like to say I forgave, but it's too hard to forget even though I've done everything to try to make things peaceful around here."

"Sounds like you need space, and I'm going to give that to you."

"So, you think it's wise to leave me here, alone, with Niriya across the way? Are you trying to push us together?"

"Oh, you having thoughts?"

"No, but you ain't helping matters any."

"Hmm…"

"What's that for?"

"Seeing her naked got you thinking, huh?"

"You think that's the first time I saw her naked?"

"Excuse me?"

"It ain't the first time. I just never told you. She came on to me before, but I didn't say anything because I already knew there was tension between you two."

"Regardless, that is something you should have told me, but it's cool. Hey, I'm just gone pack a suitcase and stay at a hotel for a couple of weeks. Apparently, you need space, and right now, so do I."

"No, what you gone do is stay here and handle your problems, and you won't do it alone. I will be here with you every step of the way. We are going to get through this together. I don't care what you say," he said as he took her keys to her car.

"But…"

"But nothing. Now, I'm going to work, but I will be back. We will pick this back up when I get home. I will try not to work late, but I do expect for you to be here when I get back tonight," he said as he grabbed her and hugged her and kissed her on her forehead.

Victoria plopped on their bed like a two-year-old child. Raymond went on about his way. She just sulked. Although Niriya got whooped by her sister, she still went home happy, knowing she caused havoc in her sister's household. This is what she lived for and what caused Victoria to have her leave in the first place. Victoria didn't know what to do. Although she has tried to avoid it, Victoria knew that she would have to face her fears. Nothing she was doing could stop Niriya.

Sowing & Reaping

Months after the Niriya incident, things around the house between Raymond and Victoria grew worse. Niriya blocked any progress Victoria had with Nigel but ensured his relationship with his father blossomed into something beautiful. Raymond didn't see how things were going from bad to worse for Victoria. Niriya designed the diversion of her plan to destroy Victoria. Although they had the talk about his love for her, Raymond's actions fortified Victoria's insecurities. He totally ignored what Victoria was going through when she wasn't around but would protect her in front of her face. He really didn't deal with how he felt about what Victoria did to his son. He wouldn't face it, and it was spewing out in various ways.

You can always tell if you've truly forgiven someone. Forgiveness flows through the body, the mind, the soul, and actions. If your actions are contrary to what forgiveness is, then you haven't truly forgiven. You can't be scared to confront the issue, even if it has to do with someone you love. You have to talk to that person; be upfront about how you feel. That is the only way healing can begin.

Raymond has yet to figure that out. The way he treats his wife proves that his forgiveness is a lie. He's even taken steps to get closer to Niriya. Nigel is digging it. He's never had a two-parent household, and what a joy it would be to have both his parents under the same roof. The more Victoria tried, the more Raymond moved closer to Niriya and Nigel. He spent more time over their house than at his own. Victoria would fix dinner, but she ended up eating alone while he ate with his son and baby mama at their home. After months of this, Victoria left. She packed up a suitcase and headed towards Savannah, GA. She didn't have anywhere to go because her parents were dead, and her closest friend was in arm's length of Raymond. She didn't want to be found. She didn't even tell Leigha she was leaving. Victoria didn't say bye to anybody. She didn't know what she would do because all she had was credit cards and $3,000 to her name. She didn't work, but she was gifted in interior decorating.

The day she left; he hadn't called her at all. That was another thing; his daily phone calls were becoming less and less. Niriya would text her the conversations and chats she would have with Raymond. Niriya talked to Raymond more than he spoke to his wife.

Anyway, the day Victoria left, Raymond saw her pull out the driveway on his way from Niriya's house. He waited for her to leave so he could go home. When he got home, he saw that all the lights were off, which was odd because she always left on a light or two even when she would leave home. He turned on the lights to see the pictures of him and his wife taken off the walls, the kitchen cleaned, and thought to himself, "She's so dramatic. Man, what a drama queen." He headed upstairs to take a shower and settle in as not to give in to the "drama queen," but when he opened the door to his bedroom, he turned on the light, and all he saw was a letter on the bed. He sat down and opened it up, and it read…

"Dear Raymond, I'm sorry, but I just can't take it anymore. You've made your choice, but I don't have to live with it nor suffer through it. Don't come looking for me because you won't find me. I didn't come to this decision lightly; it was hard. I love you with all my heart, and I thought after our "love" talk, you loved me too, but I see now I was wrong. Niriya has won. I'm not happy about it, but you gave her the winning hand she needed. In the envelope this letter came in, you will see all the texts, photos, and conversations you've had with Niriya…SHE SENT THEM TO ME EVERY TIME. You've talked with her more and took more pictures with her than you have with me for the past few months. She's all on social media with it. I get messages and texts from people asking if we're still together because she got you all posted on all her platforms. I'm tired. I may have done wrong, but it's only so much punishment I can take. I can't even believe I'm writing this…bye, Raymond.

After reading the letter and looking at all the contents in the envelope, he was furious. He tried calling Victoria, but she had his number blocked. While trying various phone calls to find his wife, Niriya sent a text; Why'd you leave? You usually stay and watch a movie with us before going home. He didn't reply. What he really wanted to do was go over there and punch her in the face, but because he was so mad and it was a school night, he stayed home and decided to confront her tomorrow while Nigel is at school. He didn't want him to be around and didn't want him to know what was going on because he was already having a hard time in his new school. Public school wasn't working even though he's only been in school for four and a half months. Nigel has already been in three fights, but he refuses to tell his parents the reasons.

Raymond was in turmoil and couldn't sleep. He tried using OnStar to track Victoria but she turned off the service on her car. She was not trying to be found by any means. He called Leigha, but she didn't have any information to give him and was furious that she would just leave like that, but Victoria didn't tell her because she was embarrassed. Now, they are both looking for her.

Hours passed, and Victoria arrived in Savannah and checked into a hotel. She paid cash as not to be traced. She made up her mind to look for a place to live and find a job tomorrow. She was in unrest. She never thought her life would turn out like this.

Raymond returned home and laid in the bed, wondering what had happened. He replayed the last few months over and over in his head. The last time he cried was when his mom passed, but now, tears fill his eyes once again. The woman he loved left. His heart was gone. He had no words, and all feelings in his body went numb. He couldn't get up to go to work the next day. He laid by his phone, hoping Victoria would call, but she didn't, though she wanted to. He tried calling her to see if she had unblocked his number. All strength was gone from him. He didn't even have enough strength to confront Niriya. She tried calling and texting him numerous times, but he never answered nor replied. He was supposed to help Nigel with his homework but he couldn't. Niriya noticed Victoria's car was gone all night and all day.

When Nigel got home from school, she told him to see if his father was home. Nigel did as his mother asked. He looked around and yelled throughout the house, "Pop! You home? Pop!" Raymond didn't answer. He walked upstairs, opened the door, and saw his father asleep next to his phone. He also saw the letter Victoria wrote and the tormenting texts and photos his mother sent her. He left everything as it was and went back home. He told his mother that his dad was fine and just sleeping. He told her he would be back because he was going over to his friend's house, and he kept his key to his dad's house on him. Niriya didn't think anything of it and let him hang out while she cooked and prepared for Raymond to come over like he has done every day for the past few months. When Nigel got far enough away from home, he called Victoria. She saw the phone ring and who it was and contemplated answering it. She decided not to pick up. Then Nigel texted her: It's me. No one knows I'm calling. She hesitated but called him back.

"Victoria, where are you?"

"I'm not in Jacksonville. Are you okay? Do you need anything?"

"No, I'm not okay. Why would you leave?"

"Nigel, you don't want me there. Why do you even care?"

"I do want you here, and I do care. I care that Pop is lying in bed next to his phone in the same clothes he wore yesterday. He's not answering the phone or texts. He didn't even go to work today."

"Okay."

"Don't be like that cause you love Pop."

"I do, but I can't do it anymore."

"I saw what my mom did to you, and that wasn't cool."

"That's just your mom. I've come to terms with that."

"Please come back."

"To what, Nigel? I can't."

"Even for me?"

"I didn't think you liked me. I'm sure you hate me because you didn't help matters any."

"Yeah, I know, but I can't stand to see Pop like this."

"I'm not feeling great either. I'm hurting too. I'm sorry. I gotta go, but please don't tell anyone you talked to me. If you call me, I will answer but only to talk to you. I don't want to talk to your mom or your dad."

"Okay. I won't. Victoria?"

"Yes."

"For what it's worth, I'm sorry."

"Thank you, sweetheart. I am too."

Days turned into weeks, weeks turned into four months, and nothing changed. Niriya wasn't letting up and using this time of Victoria's absence as an excellent time to capture Raymond. He was a mess. He hadn't talked to his wife since she left. He searches for her every day. He's sick, and his work is suffering. Niriya is taking care of him, making sure he eats, goes to work, and keeps him in close proximity to Nigel.

Victoria was in this by herself, and she lost ground, but she got a job at a warehouse factory until she can get a better job. Anything would do for now because she needed a place to live. However, she regrets leaving. She missed her husband, and Nigel kept her in the loop about everything, which made her want to go back even more, but she wasn't sure if going back was the right thing to do. Victoria wasn't sure if anything would change. What battles would she have to face because, frankly, she was tired of fighting. Nigel was really worried about his dad. He just got him back in his life; he didn't want to lose him again. Raymond was losing weight and looking sickly. Niriya still sent social media messages to Victoria, constantly mocking her for not being able to have children. She was the only one who had a son by the only man Victoria loved. This really cut her low. It cut her so low that it made her sick. Victoria began to gain excessive weight; her hair was falling out, and depression was her way of living. She was withering away.

Nigel saw what his mother was doing to his dad and Victoria, and as much as he didn't like what Victoria did to him and his mom, he couldn't watch this anymore. He didn't like what it was doing to his father. The holidays sucked because nobody was happy except Niriya. She loved the demise of her sister.

One day Raymond picked up Nigel from school. Nigel made up his mind to tell his father the secret he's been holding on to for months. He got in the car and said, "Hey, pop."

"Hey, son. How was school?"

"It was a'ight."

Raymond didn't say anything, just nodded his head.

"Dad, I got something to tell you."

"Can it wait?"

"No."

"Is it about school?"

"No."

"Then why can't it wait?"

"Because it's about Victoria."

Raymond looked up, pulled over, stopped the car, and asked, "What about Victoria?"

"I've been talking to her since she's been gone."

"What! I thought you said she blocked you too."

"That's what I told you because she didn't want me to tell anyone that I talked with her."

"Son, why would you keep something like that from me? You saw me looking for my wife, and this whole time you knew where she was."

"I don't know where she is because she won't tell me. We just talk on the phone. She told me she wouldn't block my number so I can call her if I need to."

"Give me your phone."

"She's not home. She's at work right now."

"Work?"

"Yes, she got a job."

"What time does she get off?"

"6:00."

"You're going to stay at my house tonight, so I can talk to her without your mother being around."

"Okay, Pop, but don't hurt Victoria anymore. She's going through it too."

When Raymond got home, he told Niriya that he wanted Nigel to stay with him for the night to have some father-son time. She bucked for a minute but finally gave in; truthfully, she just wanted to be with them. Raymond was anxious because he had no idea what he was going to say to his wife. Since the end of last year, he hasn't spoken to her, and now it's the beginning of March. He doesn't even know how to act. He doesn't know how to feel. 7:00 rolled around, and he figured she had enough time to get settled in after work, so they called her, but there wasn't an answer. They called again at 7:15, with no answer, and again at 7:30, there was still no answer. Nigel said, "That's not like her. She always answers my calls even if she has to text me that she'll call me right back." Raymond said, "We'll try again at 8:30. They ate dinner, worked on Nigel's homework, then 8:30

rolled around. They called no answer. Raymond asked, "Did you tell her that you told me?" Nigel answered, "No, Pops, I didn't." They tried calling her again at 9 but to no avail. They got ready for bed and went to sleep since there wasn't anything more they could do at this point. Nigel figured she had to work over because they made her sometimes, and that's what he told his dad. It was 1:30 in the morning, and Nigel's phone rang. He looked at it and saw it was Victoria. He answered and said, "Hey, Victoria, I've been trying to call you all night."

"Hello, is this Nigel?" a man's voice on the other end of the call asked.

"Yeah, who dis?" Nigel asked.

"My name is SGT Taylor, and I'm calling because Mrs. Victoria has you down as an emergency contact on her phone."

"What's wrong? Is Victoria okay?"

"How old are you, Nigel?"

"Why?"

"You sound kind of young."

"I'm her stepson, and I'm 15," Nigel answered as he got out of bed to go to his father's room to wake him up.

"Okay. Is there an adult I can speak to?"

"Hold on, I'm waking up my dad." Nigel walked over to his father, shaking him, saying, "Pop, wake up. It's an emergency."

"What's wrong?" Raymond asked.

"The police is calling from Victoria's phone."

"What! Hello," Raymond said, taking the phone from Nigel.

"Hello, my name is SGT Taylor. With whom am I speaking?"

"Raymond, Victoria is my wife. What's going on, Officer?"

"Victoria has been in a serious car accident."

"What happened?"

"A drunk driver jumped the median and hit her head-on. The car flipped over, and we had to use the jaws of life to get her out of the car. The good thing is she will live."

"Where is she? What hospital?"

"Memorial Hospital."

"Memorial? Where's that?"

"On Waters Ave."

"Waters Ave? Where's that?

"Savannah, GA."

"Savannah? Wow."

"Yes, Savannah. Did you not know she was here?"

"No, I didn't. Do you have a number where I can reach you when we get there?"

"Sure. It's 912-355-8747."

"Here's my number in case anything else happens 904-742-5329. And again, my name is Raymond," he said, then they hung up the phone.

Raymond jumped up and told Nigel to pack some clothes so they could hit the road. He was puzzled about Victoria being in Savannah and didn't know how to feel about the whole thing. He was just ready to be by his wife's bedside. They left without even letting Niriya know they had left. Raymond didn't even think about it until Nigel mentioned it. He told him they will call her in the morning and let her know what is happening. He wasn't worried about Nigel missing school since it was Friday. He wasn't sure he was even going to tell Niriya the whole truth, but he'll figure that out once he gets there.

After a couple hours on the road, they arrived at Memorial Hospital. They found out what room she was in and headed that way. When they got to the nurse's station, he asked for an update on his wife. Once he showed them proof of who he was they filled him in on her injuries. He walked in and saw his wife in bandages and blood. She was asleep. He stared at her at first, looked at her leg in a cast, wraps around her head, bruises on her face, but he dared not lift up the bedsheets to see her broken ribs. He didn't want her to know he was there. He pulled up a chair beside her, and he and

Nigel slept. Six o'clock rolled around, and they woke Victoria up to get her vitals. The nurse said, "Looks like you have some guests." Victoria turned her head and saw her husband and Nigel and said, "I guess I do." The nurse said, "He was so worried about you when he came in and never left your side." Victoria replied, "That's my, Ray." Then Raymond woke up after hearing all the beeping of the machines. He saw Victoria with her eyes open and started to speak but felt a lack of words, so he stroked her hand instead and kept kissing her hand. Then Nigel woke up and saw her eyes open and rushed to hug her. "Be careful, honey. She has broken ribs," the nurse said as Victoria let out a slow grunt in pain. "I'm sorry, Victoria." She said, "It's okay, sweetheart." The nurse finished checking her vitals, left the room, and closed the door. Raymond said, "Ria…I…I'm…I'm never letting you out of my sight again. I'm going to spend my life taking care of you the right way." Victoria didn't say a word because her tears spoke for her. She's been ready to go home to see her husband and to hear his words gave her the release she needed.

Mid-morning, Raymond called Leigha and told her what happened. He gave Victoria the phone to give Leigha a chance to speak with her. He also called Niriya but not in the room with Victoria. He told her that he wanted to take Nigel away for a man's weekend. She was trippin' at first but saw there was nothing she could do about it, so she left it alone. He "schooled" Nigel on what he told his mom so their stories would align. The doctor told Raymond that it was going to be either a week or more, depending on Victoria's vitals so he thought it best to take Nigel back. Since it was only about an hour and a half back to Jacksonville, he took Nigel back home Sunday night as to not let on, to Niriya, that anything was happening.

After being in the hospital for a week, they released Victoria, and it was time for her to go home. During her stay, Raymond took care of Victoria's affairs, including her job and the extended-stay hotel where she lived. He hated to see how she was living. He thought to himself, "It must have really been bad at home for her to come here and live in this kind of place. She'd rather live here than at home? I've got to change some things." Nigel was glad Victoria was coming home. He hadn't seen his dad with a smile on his face in a long time. It looked like things were going to get back to normal. It would be a long road, but they were all up for the fight by now.

After the long drive home, Raymond pulled up in the driveway, and of course, Niriya was watching her window to see when they would be home. When she looked out the window, she saw Victoria getting out of the car and Raymond putting her in a wheelchair. She hated to see her sister back but was glad to see she was hurt. She has absolutely no love for her sister, and she feels no remorse. The only thing she realized was that Raymond would focus all his energy on her and not come over as much. Victoria was not able to go upstairs to their bedroom because of her broken leg. So, Raymond made the downstairs guestroom their temporary bedroom until she heals. Their house was big enough to where he didn't have to make significant changes because of her condition. The estranged couple had a lot to recover from, but Victoria's health is their first priority.

Raymond was so worried about his wife that the big production he was overseeing was falling short to the point where he is close to being fired. Their pastor and co-pastor called and checked on them from time to time and consistently prayed for Evang Victoria. Eventually, Nigel became even more worried about Victoria, and he saw how his father agonized over her condition. He never wanted to see Victoria like that. As time went by, Nigel began to care for Victoria during the time she was gone, and it continued to grow as he helped his father take care of her. He would sneak over soup for her because his mother would have a fit if she knew what he was doing. He would also write her poems and put them on her nightstand next to her side of the bed.

The last poem he sent to her this morning (while spending the weekend with them) said, "I know you worry. I know you hurt. I know you have indescribable pain, and depression is what you exert. But I want to let you know that I care for you, and love is what you are due. I pray that God blesses you with your heart's desire and that once again, you will feel that Holy Ghost fire. I'm sorry for all that I put you through and for what my mom has done too. But if you would only smile for me, my heart would leap. Love Nigel."

Victoria cried. She knew she couldn't let Niriya know all that Nigel had been doing for her, but this poem broke her down. I touched Nigel's heart for Victoria while he's been attending church with his dad. I've been breaking him down little by little. Victoria placed his poem in her Bible. Only Nigel knew how depressed she was while healing and even before she left his dad. It became worse after the accident. She can't move like she wants to, stuck in the house until Raymond gets off work, her sister hasn't called or come by to see her, and she and Raymond still haven't had "the talk." She texted Nigel while he was in school, and it said, "Thank you, Nigel. Thank you so much. I really needed this." Nigel texted back: I meant every word I said. Then she sent him a virtual gif hug and said, "I won't say anything to your mom because I know she wouldn't like this at all." He texted back, "You know my mama." For the time being, Victoria and Nigel kept their getting along with each other a secret. Victoria felt a little better, but she still longed for a child of her own. Here is Victoria, another year and a half came and went and with no baby nor a sign of one coming soon.

After six weeks, Victoria was healed and the cast was taken off but she and Raymond still had to face the issues in their marriage before she left. They've continuously ignored the elephant in the room. Nothing had changed in that regard. They would take trips to the pond or the lake to think and rekindle the flame and get away from the stresses of home, pretending as if everything was okay.

It's been a year and they still avoided the conversation. Raymond didn't want to talk about it since mentally, his wife was still in a fragile place. Victoria hasn't driven at all since the wreck because she has flashbacks from the accident. The drunk driver didn't get much time because it was his first offense. He only had to spend six months in jail. She did receive a nice sum settlement though. Her car was totaled, of course, but she never purchased another vehicle. If Raymond can't drive her or Leigha can't pick her up, she doesn't go anywhere. Raymond's work performance was still suffering. Niriya is still kicking up dust. Victoria's cast wasn't off two seconds before Niriya started up with her shenanigans again. She was making things difficult at Raymond's job and at home. She has people at his job thinking he's having an affair by calling him and leaving messages saying that she's his girlfriend. Mrs. Steppleton would take the messages and give them to Raymond, but she lost all respect for him. She is a married woman and does not tolerate adultery. He's tried to tell her that it's not what it is, but Niriya makes it very convincing. She even visits his job all dolled up, walks into his office, and then leaves looking disheveled as if to suggest they just finished having sex. It looked like he had no control over his home and none over his job. Everything was out of control.

While all this was happening, the home environment was affecting Nigel at school. Raymond kept him at public school because he didn't think it was fair to move him due to what was happening at home. His grades aren't the best. He's not fighting as much anymore, mainly because he could fight, and they didn't want to keep messing with him. The boys in the neighborhood were having an impact on him. He wanted to do better. They don't get into trouble, and they work hard. He's having thoughts about transferring schools his junior year to be with them.

Victoria thought things would change if she came back, but things worsened because she still hasn't faced her fears nor her past. Raymond is doing a lot better, though but he's fed up that his wife still won't put Niriya in her place. He's on the verge of losing his job because his home life shows up at work. They have some decisions to make before disobedience and running from fears cost them everything.

Reality vs Recovery

"For the last two years, I've been battling, going through so bad, having ups and downs. My marriage is holding on by mere threads. And Niriya continues to go after my husband. The only thing keeping me going is Nigel; isn't that ironic? I keep trying to snap out of this funk but constantly find myself going back in. It's been rough, but today is my forty-fifth birthday, and I've decided I'm going to enjoy it," Victoria thought to herself as she walked with her husband up to her favorite restaurant.

"Surprise! Happy Birthday, Victoria!" Raymond, Nigel, Leigha, Joshua, and other associates yelled in this classy, upscale restaurant for a surprise party that Raymond set up for her.

"Oh, my gawd! Thank you," Victoria said in shock.

"Happy Birthday, sweetheart," Raymond said, kissing his wife on the cheek.

"I love you, Ray," Victoria said.

Nigel hugged her and whispered in her ear, "Happy Birthday, Mom." She hugged him so tight and cried.

"What did you say to her, Nigel," Raymond asked, thinking he said something to her sideways.

"It's our little secret," Victoria said to Raymond. Nigel smiled and took a seat.

"Yeah, ease up, Pops," Nigel said.

"Happy Birthday, gurl," Leigha said as she hugged her best friend.

"You are too much," Victoria said.

"Happy birthday Vic!" Joshua said.

"Thanks, Joshua," said Victoria.

"Come on, everybody, let's have a seat and get ready to eat," Raymond said.

Everyone sat down and ordered their food. Intimate conversations, laughter, and jokes were going on at the table. Victoria had a corner full of gifts from her family and friends. After everyone finished their entrée, Raymond signaled the waitress to bring in the cake. In walks, the waitress with a strawberry-glazed yellow cake with the lit candle numbers four and five on it. Everyone sang happy birthday to Victoria. When it was time for her to blow out the candles, she said, "Thank you guys for making my forty-fifth birthday a happy one. I hadn't enjoyed a decent birthday in years. I've spent those times crying and wallowing in my troubles, but today you have caused me to smile, so…thank you so much." She paused for a few seconds, then blew out the candles. Each person began to clap their hands because they knew all she had gone through. As soon as all of them stopped clapping, in walks Victoria's arch enemy.

"Don't stop clapping for me," Niriya said.

Raymond stood up, walked over, and said in a deep and quiet tone, "Today is not the day. Go home and leave my wife alone."

"Not likely," Niriya said.

Nigel got up and said, "Ma, come on. Don't do this."

"Oh, so you on her side now?" Niriya said.

"It's not like that, Ma. We are in a nice restaurant, and there's no need for this," Nigel said.

Before she could respond to Nigel, Leigha walked over and said, "Baebae, you got tha right one. I'd suggest you bounce right now or get bounced."

"Please, you put no fear in my heart. Sit down and shut up, you ghetto hood rat," Niriya said.

"Did she just say ghetto hood rat?" Leigha said looking back at Victoria as Joshua held her back.

"Chill out, Leigha," Joshua said.

"Let me go! You ain't my man!" Leigha said.

Joshua let her go, and Raymond looked at him like, "What's up with that?" Then Joshua said, "You're right."

"Shut up!" Leigh yelled again, losing control.

"You better be careful using that word being the fact that your friend's womb is shut," Niriya said loud enough for Victoria to hear and embarrass her.

Just then, Leigha pulled back, clenched her fist, swung on Niriya with all that was within her, and knocked her out cold. By her doing that, Niriya caused two tables to collapse, and glass flew everywhere. Raymond bowed down to make sure that Niriya was okay. She woke up a few moments later. Leigha went back to her chair and sat down with no remorse and a smile on her face. Niriya ended up leaving, but she made a scene before she left, "You will pay for that! I'm pressing charges against you."

"Yeah, and I will press charges of harassment," Victoria said as she stood up and walked towards Niriya.

"I got what I came for, so I will leave," Niriya said as she exited the excluded backroom where the party was being held.

"What did she mean by that?" Raymond asked.

"You know she's up to something," Victoria replied.

They all left soon after the "drama," and frankly, I was tired of Niriya myself, but as long as Victoria allows her to continue to do what she wants to do, then nothing will change. Raymond and Victoria went home and were soon asleep. As Victoria rested, I gave her a dream. "Hi, sweetheart," Victoria said as she held a baby boy in her arms. She stood on a beach with her feet clinching the sand. She walked towards the body of water that is a perfect color of teal green, and the rays from the sun caused it to look crystallized. Soon after, there was a push, and Victoria dropped the baby in the water. When she looked back to see who had pushed her, there was no one there that she could see, but she could feel a strong force behind her. As she looked back towards the sea, she saw the baby boy drifting away by the waves. The baby was crying, and Victoria tried to run and get him, but she couldn't because that strong force pulled her away from the water. "Noooo! Let me go! I've got to save my baby! Let me go!" Victoria screamed with desperation.

"Let me go!" Victoria yelled in her sleep.

"Baby, baby, wake up," Raymond said as he shook her.

"Huh…wha...what," Victoria woke up with tears in her eyes.

"Ria, are you alright, sweetheart?"

"I just had a bad dream."

"Are you crying?"

"It was a nightmare."

"What was it about?"

Victoria told Raymond the dream. She couldn't even finish it without shedding more tears. As she told him this, he saw the dream in a vision. I showed him vividly. When she finished the dream, I started to show him what the dream meant.

"Ray, I have no clue what it means…if it even has a meaning."

"It means something, Ria."

"What does it mean?"

"The dream has multiple meanings. The first meaning is the baby boy is your promise, and you had him in your hands, but then someone who doesn't want you to receive your promise caused you to drop him. You couldn't see the person because you didn't want to see the person behind you and this force wants to keep you from the promise. Did the baby die in the dream?"

"No, he stayed above water the whole time…even after the waves kept tossing him. All the baby did was cry."

"Your promise isn't dead yet, but it's in dangerous waters, and if you don't handle this force that's behind you, you will eventually lose your promise."

"What is this force?"

"You already know the answer to that in your heart. God has shown it to you. You may be able to hide things from me but never from Him."

"What is that supposed to mean?"

"God has shown it to you and has even had strangers and family to tell you what the force is."

"How did you know?"

"I am your husband, and God does show me things. You know there ain't much that He doesn't let me know about."

"I guess."

"The baby in the dream represents promises. God didn't only promise you a baby, but the other promises are a restored marriage and what He's called you to do. This force is threatening everything about your life. It's threatening our marriage and the business He has called you to open, and you're allowing it by not handling things on your end."

"You saw all that?"

"No, that's what God showed me."

"Uhm…"

"What do you think this dream is about?"

"That I need to do something about Niriya."

"Victoria, you have put it off for years, and because of your fear of her, you refuse to handle it and put an end to all this drama. Haven't you had enough? When are you going to take your life back?"

"It's so much more to it, Raymond."

"What, does she have something else on you?"

"No, but it does stem from our childhood."

"What else could there be?"

"I don't want to talk about it right now."

"Well, as long as you don't get whatever it is right, the longer it will be to take hold of your promise if you take hold of it at all. Go back to sleep if you can. I love you."

"I love you too."

Raymond kissed his wife on the cheek, rolled over, and went back to sleep. Victoria rolled over too, but she couldn't fall back to sleep. There was a lot on her mind. She stared off into the darkness of her room, and all she could see was Niriya's face and Niriya laughing at her. Victoria finally knew what Niriya meant when she said she got what she came for at her birthday party. Victoria eventually fell back to sleep, but by the time she did, it was only another hour before she had to wake back up.

The next morning Raymond got himself ready for work. He wasn't feeling work as he once did, and it was taking its toll. He believed it was time for him to do something else. His heart wasn't at his job anymore. He can't identify the problem and where it went array. Yet, he knew he had a status to uphold and a wife that enjoys the benefits of the high lifestyle, so he stays. Victoria noticed a change in her husband too. He wasn't gung-ho about going to work. Little did Raymond know, I talked to Victoria as well. She isn't an evangelist for nothing.

"Are you okay, Raymond?" Victoria asked.

"I'm fine," Raymond said.

"Are you sure?"

"Yes. Why are you asking?"

"Well, lately, you seem unmotivated when getting ready for work."

"Is it that obvious?"

"Uh, yeah."

"I don't know why I'm feeling like this."

"Could it be that you haven't listened to the Lord?"

"What are you talking about?"

"Raymond, you know what I'm talking about."

"No, I don't. Explain it to me."

"How long has it been since God told you to open your company?"

"Years."

"Well…what are you waiting for?"

"I don't know."

"It's always been your dream to start your own productions company. You have all the talent, know-how, background, and you also have a master's degree. Need I say that money isn't an issue either?"

"I don't know, Victoria."

"How long will you continue to force yourself to go to a job that your heart isn't in anymore?"

"Maybe I'm just in a rut. I'll come out of it."

"Or maybe you just need to go ahead and do it, but hey, take all the time you need."

"Just like you?"

"What is that supposed to mean?"

"Just what it sounded like."

"Oh, so we are doing it like that now? I was trying to do was encourage you but don't worry about it."

Raymond paused and exhaled and asked, "Why have we been arguing so much lately?"

"I don't know. It's been pretty tense around here."

"How can we turn this around, Victoria?"

"Bottom line…we gotta do what God is telling us to do. Both of us have failed in that area, and until we get that straight, nothing will work."

"What are you willing to do?"

"Ray, it's not about what I am willing to do. It's about what are WE willing to do."

"Should we go to counseling?"

"Counseling, for what? I just told you how to solve the problem. Why would I waste my time when I already know what I have to do? In the end, it boils down to us being obedient."

"I was just asking Victoria. I still believe we could benefit from counseling."

"Well, Raymond, I just answered. And I'm not going to sit in front of anybody else so they can evaluate what a bad person I am. We know what we need to do and need to just do it."

"Man, we are getting nowhere."

Raymond walked out of the house and went to work. He was confused, mad, irritated, and still not motivated. He was lost and didn't know where to be found. Meanwhile, Victoria made up her mind that she was going to put a stop to Niriya's plans once and for all. Victoria came up with her own agenda. She worked diligently for a week to put everything in place. She made phone calls, set up people, places, and things. Victoria has mad connections, and she used them all to handle Niriya. It was about to be on.

One month later, Victoria had everything set in place, and it was all about to go down. Raymond had no idea what Victoria was about to pull off. Within that month, she was out of town to various cities. Her husband didn't even ask what all the trips were about. He was caught up in his own miserable world.

One afternoon, Niriya and Nigel were relaxing and talking to each other, having a family day together. School was about to start for Nigel. He talked with his dad about switching schools, and his dad was happy to register him for private school. He's starting his junior year at the academy and looking forward to hanging with his neighborhood friends. Niriya couldn't get him ready for it financially because she didn't have a job. Raymond and Victoria bought all that he needed for school. Victoria took him school shopping while Niriya was doing the registration work. She couldn't stand what Victoria was doing for him, and she had a feeling that he was beginning to like her. He would usually fuss not to go with her; now, he doesn't. Little did she know that the antics she was pulling showed him that Victoria wasn't so bad; his mother was causing the problems. The fact that Victoria took everything that her sister was doing showed Nigel a lot about her character. He couldn't stay mad with her because he kind of understood why she did what she did. However, Nigel still wanted to talk with his mother and Victoria about what happened years ago.

Around three in the afternoon, Niriya received a phone call, "Hello."

"May I speak to Niriya James?" the person on the other end of the phone call asked.

"This is she. Who is this?" Niriya asked.

"My name is Terry Swan, and I'm with Regal and Regal Accounts. I have your resume that you put in a while ago, and I wanted to call you in for an interview," he said.

"Regal and Regal Accounts? I don't remember sending my resume," she said.

"Are you Niriya James?" Terry asked.

"Yes," she answered.

"Do you live at 5673 Mosaic Blvd?" he continued.

"Yes," she said.

"You graduated with an Associate's from Chancellor University?"

"Yes, but it's just strange that…,"

"You have an impressive resume. Would you be able to come in for an interview?"

"Sure."

"How about Monday at 10:00 a.m.?"

"That sounds great. Where exactly are you located?"

"We are at 1005 Lincoln Dr. Do you know where the old, shut-down theater is?"

"Yes."

"We are four blocks from there. Once you get to the theater, turn left. Come down three traffic lights and turn right. Then you are going to make a left at the first street you come to once you make that right."

"Okay. I got it. Oh, what is the position that I'm interviewing for?"

"Secretary."

"Alright, well, I look forward to seeing you on Monday."

"Good, see you then. Have a nice day."

"You too."

They hung up the phone, and Nigel asked, "Ma, what was that all about?" "Baby! Your momma got an interview for a secretary job on Monday!" she yelled in excitement.

"That's what's up, Ma!" Nigel said as he hugged her.

They were jumping and hollering all over the living room. She was so happy, and he was just as glad for his mom. I answered his prayers. He felt like she needed a break.

Victoria left for Massachusetts earlier that morning. Therefore, she wasn't there when Nigel tried to come and tell her the good news. He called her on her cell phone instead.

"Hello, Nigel," Victoria answered.

"Where are you?" Nigel asked.

"I'm in Massachusetts," Victoria answered.

"Massachusetts? Why are you there?" he said.

"Taking care of some small matters. Are you alright?" Victoria asked as Nigel sounded confused.

"I'm good, but why didn't you tell me that you were going out of town? I've been looking for you, and you've been in and out a lot this past month," Nigel said.

"I know, and I'm sorry I didn't tell you. I have something important that I'm taking care of, and I lost track of telling you guys where I was. Sooo, what's up?" Victoria asked.

"I wanted to tell you some good news," Nigel said.

"Yeah, what's that?" she asked again.

"My mom got an interview on Monday," he said.

"That's good. I'm really happy for her," Victoria stated.

"She is so happy, Victoria," he said.

"Who is the interview with?" Victoria asked.

"I don't know. We were so excited that I didn't get around to asking her any questions," Nigel said.

"I can understand that," Victoria said.

"When are you coming back?" Nigel asked.

"Tomorrow," she answered.

"Alright, I'll see you then. I want to spend the night with you and dad tomorrow before I go back to school Monday," Nigel said.

"Okay. Where do you want to go to eat? Or would you like to have a few of your friends over for a back-to-school bash?" she asked.

"Ah, yeah! It's party time!" Nigel said.

"I knew you would like that," Victoria said snickering.

"Let me call them now so we can make some plans. Bye," he said.

"Bye," she said as they both hung up the phone.

The weekend is over and Monday was vastly approaching. Nigel was getting ready to start a new school, and Niriya was preparing for her interview. It had been a while since Niriya had a job. She could never keep one though she had a degree. She wanted to have someone to blame for her life, and Victoria was that scapegoat. She continues to blame Victoria for everything, but reality is about to hit her.

Nigel rode with his friends to school. They had cars and permits for parking at school. Nigel couldn't wait to learn to drive. Raymond and Victoria went to breakfast, and Niriya got ready for her interview. Victoria is so giddy today, so much so that Raymond couldn't help but notice. It was like she was playing poker for the first time, giving away her winning hand. She had one serious poker face. Nothing had changed much in their household, and they were pretty much going through the motions, but it was refreshing to see his wife smile for a change. As they sat down at the restaurant table, Raymond asked Victoria, "What are you so happy about?"

"Oh, nothing. I've just decided to be happy," Victoria said.

"No, I know you, and you are up to something," Raymond said.

"Nooo, I'm not," Victoria insisted.

"Hello, my name is Tammy, and I will be your waitress today. What can I get you to drink?" Tammy asked.

"I'll have a fruity lemonade," Victoria said.

"And I'll have coffee for right now," Raymond said.

"Okay, I'll be right back with your drinks," Tammy said.

"So, what do you have planned for today?" Victoria asked.

"I have a couple of meetings, then we start casting for the upcoming movie that we're producing," Raymond said.

"What is it about?" Victoria asked.

"It's another gang movie," Raymond said.

"You don't sound happy about that," Victoria said.

"I'm not. I'm tired of doing those kinds of movies. If it ain't about gangs, it's about women sleeping around or marriages that don't make it. There is no substance to it," Raymond said.

"Well, what movies would you like to do?" asked Victoria.

"I don't know…something more meaningful but not that," Raymond said.

"Here are your drinks. Are you ready to order?" Tammy asked.

"I'll have the chicken, egg, and cheese bagel," Victoria ordered.

"And I'll have pancakes, steak, and eggs and hash brown casserole," Raymond ordered.

"Did you want something else to drink other than coffee with your food?" Tammy asked.

"Yes, I'll have orange juice," Raymond answered.

"Alright, I'll be back with your food," Tammy said as she walked away.

"Raymond, why don't you do what inspires you?" Victoria said.

"What, like God's word, His stories," Raymond answered sarcastically.

"Step out on faith and start your own company. You know you are supposed to anyway so why prolong the inevitable," Victoria said.

"When you walk in faith, so will I. Now just leave that alone," he said.

"Why do you always go there? All I wanted to do was help you. I'm tired of arguing with you about all this, and I didn't come to eat breakfast with you for this either," she said.

"I'm tired of hearing you preach to me and not taking your own advice. Your witness to me is of non-effect. That is why I don't want to listen to you," he shared.

"Oh, I guess that's fair," she said.

"Can I talk to you seriously?" he asked.

"Sure," she answered.

"Have you wondered why we haven't been intimate lately?" he asked.

"I've been out of town a great deal this past month, so I haven't given it much thought, but I guess now that you've said something, I have noticed that you've been distant."

"I have lost respect for you."

"Respect for me…why?"

Tammy approached them with their order. Once she placed their food on the table, they continued this inquisitive conversation.

"I have always known you to stand up for yourself. What made me fall for you in the beginning was how you handled your business. Somehow, you've lost that, and you allow Niriya to treat you any kind of way."

"I see how you may feel that way, but you don't know the whole story of our childhood. Have you ever tried to see things from my end?"

"What end is that?"

"I sent her away years ago, and I was wrong for that, but do you see why I did?"

"Yes and no. Not only did you move her away, but you also moved my son away, and that's where you went wrong. Why didn't you keep him here?"

"Do you really want to know? Are you ready?"

"As ready as I'm going to be."

"For one, she slept with someone else, so I wasn't even sure the baby she was carrying was ours. Eventually, we got a DNA test done and found out that you were the father…."

"Wait a minute, what? Hold up…how did you get a DNA test done without me knowing about it?"

"I guess it don't matter now since I'm already knee-deep in it…"

"You finna piss me off. I can feel it."

"Since you sleep harder after we have sex, I swabbed you then. Do you remember when I convinced you to have a drink one night when we went out for date night but you really didn't want to do it?"

"Yeah, I remember that and you knew why I didn't want to do it but I did it because of you."

"You remember we spent the night at the hotel downtown after that?"

"Uh, huh."

"Well, we had a wild night…"

"Yeah, that night has been forever etched on my brain. I ain't never forgotten about that night."

"You slept real good too and that was when I swabbed you. I knew you wouldn't wake up and you made it so easy cause your mouth was wide open from snoring."

Raymond closed his eyes and shook his head as took his fingers and rubbed them on his forehead in disbelief and sighed. Then he said, "What's wrong with you females? How do you not tell me something like that? See, this is why I can't stay focused because there's always some BS poppin' off. And you talk about what you are tired of."

"I didn't want to say anything until there was something that needed to be said. It wasn't worth the extra drama."

"Whateva."

"Second, I was tired of her, and the only way to bring back the little bit of joy that I had was to move her away. I didn't think about how it would affect you, and at the time, I really didn't care. You should have seen how you were with her and Nigel. It was like I was the third wheel, but you would never admit to that. Even after all that has happened, you still haven't acknowledged your wrong in all this."

"My wrong! You've got to be kidding me."

"The last time I checked, I wasn't a comedian, so no, I'm not kidding."

"How am I at fault?"

"I didn't say that you were at fault, but I am saying that you played a part."

"And what part was that?"

"You left me out of almost everything. You didn't care about how she treated me. All you cared about was Nigel and his mother. I WAS SUPPOSED TO BE HIS MOTHER!"

"Calm down and lower your voice."

"Don't tell me to calm down! I've got every right to be upset," Victoria said, standing to her feet, slamming down the white linen napkin, and walking out.

"Victoria!" Raymond kind of whispered-yelled as to not cause more attention. He left money on the table and went after her.

"What do you want Raymond? Just take me home and go to work."

"No, no listen! You are right; I didn't see. I admit; I cared about Nigel more than I cared about you. I was just so happy I had a son Victoria."

"See how you keep saying YOU had a son. Shouldn't it have been WE had a son?"

"Baby, you are right. I don't want to fight anymore."

"Me neither. I just want to be done with this whole thing. I want to move forward. I want you to start your own company. I want us to have a baby, but I don't think it will happen for us. We can't even get ourselves together, so why would God bless us with our own child."

"Don't cry, Ria."

Raymond held his wife as she laid her head in his chest. He put her in the car to take her home. The ride home was quiet. Neither wanted to say anything. It was time to just be quiet. I was speaking to each one of their hearts. Niriya was across the way at her job interview, making a good impression. The interviewer hired her on the spot. She was excited. She couldn't wait to tell someone, but reality quickly hit her that she had so many enemies she didn't have anyone to share it with except her son, who is in school right now. Now her time of rejoicing has become bittersweet. Raymond took Victoria home and went to work. Victoria went upstairs and prayed about the whole situation.

"Father, I'm so done, so done that I don't know what to do. I'm tired of fighting, tired of crying, tired of arguing, and even tired of praying. I don't know if You hear me or if I'm not in right standing with You. I don't know what's going on, but You have got to fix this. I love my husband. You know I do, but we have been struggling for years now. We need help. What is it going to take? How much more do we have to go through?"

The telephone rang, "Hello," Victoria answered.

"Hey Victoria," Co-Pastor Riley said.

"Hi, Co-Pastor," Victoria replied.

"You've been on my heart Victoria. I called to tell you what God has given me to say. You know that Pastor and I have been praying for you and Raymond."

"Yes, I know."

"The Lord says, He can't talk to either of you because you got too much going on, but there is hope. He says it's time to be quiet. Stop arguing. Stop fussing because all that is doing is fueling the fire. When you all become quiet, He will be able to speak. He also said to read Proverbs 22:10, which says, "Cast out the scorner, and contention shall go out; yea, strife, and reproach shall cease." Victoria, make sure that you listen to what He says."

"Yes, ma'am."

"I'll see you all Sunday."

"Okay. See you then and Co-Pastor…thank you."

"Thank God, baby. He's the one doing it."

They hung up the phone. One thing about Co-Pastor Riley, she doesn't stay on the phone long. She always says what I tell her, no more, no less. I know I can trust her with the mysteries I share. She will do what she is supposed to do. My daughter knows the difference between flesh and spirit…My Spirit.

Victoria stopped praying after the phone call and went about doing her daily duties. The scripture made her smile because she quickly grasped what she had to do, and she was already putting it into action, but it wasn't the action I wanted her to take. She misunderstood the scripture as many of my children do. However, Victoria always seems to shut down after a word. She doesn't understand why she does that. I will reveal it to her in time, though. While Raymond is at work, he has difficulty staying focused, so his boss called him into the office.

"Raymond, what is going on with you?" said Mr. Balstic.

"What do you mean?" Raymond asked.

"You have been off your game for a while now. I thought you would come out of it, but you haven't. I don't know what is going on with you, but you have to get it together. We cannot lose this account. It's one of the biggest ones we have. Joshua has been picking up your slack, and that's not fair to him that he has to pull your weight and his," Mr. Balstic said.

"You're right, Mr. Balstic. I'm sorry, but I've had a lot going on since I found my son. I never thought it would be like this, but I'm going to get back on my game," Raymond said.

"I'm sorry to hear that, but you can't bring home to work. I like you, Raymond, and you do great work, but I've had Fred threaten to leave, and I can't let that happen. In saying that, I'm giving Joshua the account and putting you on leave. You have a few weeks to fix home and come back ready to work," said Mr. Balstic.

"I understand, Mr. Balstic. You gotta do what you gotta do," Raymond said upset but relieved.

"Don't be like that, Raymond. You know I've done all I can. But Dolan Productions is a huge account. We've worked with them for years, and I'm not going to lose it because one of my employees can't separate work from home," Mr. Balstic replied.

"It's cool, Mr. Balstic. I'll straighten out my home, and I'll be ready to work when I come back…full force," Raymond said.

"That's what I like to hear," Mr. Balstic said, shaking Raymond's hand with a smile.

Raymond walked to his office to get his things and go home. He really didn't know how to feel about it all. Joshua saw Raymond in his office and said, "Hey, man, is everything okay?"

"Mr. Balstic put me on leave because apparently, I can't separate home from work," Raymond said.

"What is he going to do about Dolan Productions?" Fred has been a thorn in my side with all his crazy demands. Mr. Balstic doesn't know how tedious this has been," said Joshua.

"Well, it's about to get worse my brotha because he is placing you over the account," Raymond said.

"Man, are you serious?"

"Yes, I am."

"How long are you going to be gone?"

"Just a couple of weeks."

"Weeks! Come on, man. Can we do something about this?"

"Joshua, I don't know how to feel about it either. I'm upset, but then again, I'm not. I almost feel free."

"I bet you do cause you don't have to deal with these people," Joshua said as they both laughed.

"Victoria keeps telling me that I need to open my own company and do the work God created me to do," Raymond said.

"Yeah, what happened with that because I remember you talking about it a while back? I didn't think anything more about it because you didn't do anything with it. Well, if you need somebody, I'm your man."

"I don't know what I'm going to do. I guess I'll have to pray about it, and you know I got to have my number one man on the job."

"I'm ya boi."

"Alright, man, let me go, and you get to work."

"Can I call you if I need help?"

"Yeah, man, you know I got you, but you've been doing this for a long time, so I know you got it."

"Thanks, man," said Joshua leaving the office.

"No problem," Raymond said.

Raymond got into his car and started to head home but decided to take a detour. He went out to the beach, which was about thirty minutes from his house. He didn't call Victoria and tell her about anything that was going on. Instead, he enjoyed the rest of the day on the beach. He sat and looked back over everything that had happened over the past two to three years. Raymond realized he had allowed these situations to dictate his relationship with Me. I wish he would believe I don't just punish my children for delaying and disobeying. My mercies are new every morning. True, I don't let it go on for a length of time because, at one time or another, he is going to have to anny-up.

As he watched the waters come to shore and recede back into the ocean, a revelation hit him. A little girl was writing in the sand, but it wiped away whatever she wrote when the water crashed upon the shore. I gave him the thought, "God can wash away whatever we write into our lives that shouldn't be in an instant, and we have to be willing to let it go." He finally saw what Victoria was talking about. "We wrote Niriya into our lives because we weren't patient with the promise God gave us twenty years ago. I have to be willing to let her go, and if that means Nigel, I'll do what I have to do as his father and be there for him the best I can, but Niriya has got to go." He understood what he had to do, but little did he know that Victoria already had plans in place.

Niriya came home, and she wanted so bad to tell her sister about her new job. However, she knows Victoria doesn't want anything to do with her other than Nigel. She figured that she would tell Nigel when he gets home from school, and Victoria will find out that way. Soon after, Nigel came home from school, but he didn't seem so happy, but he was excited to find out how his mom's interview went.

"Hey, Ma," Nigel said.

"Hey, baby, what is going on?" Niriya asked, realizing that something was going on with her son.

"Nothing, Ma," Nigel answered.

"I know when something is going on with my baby. Come on now, speak up," Niriya said.

"I just don't like my school. I thought I would because of my friends, but I don't. Those other kids are stuck-up, and you know I don't rock like that. I know dad wants me to get a good education, but it ain't me. That school just ain't me, Ma," Nigel said.

"I know because you are used to public schools but stick it out because this will be better for you," Niriya said.

"That's what everyone keeps saying, but this neighborhood ain't me. The school ain't me. This whole lifestyle ain't me. I thought I would want to live like tha stars, but I feel out of place," Nigel said.

"Son give it some time," Niriya said.

"But Ma, I've lived here for two years, and I still feel out of place. How much time do I have to give it?"

"You will get used to it, trust me. Give the school a chance."

"I thought leaving my old school would be better, but I just want to go back."

"Just stick it out because you only have two more years of school, and you will have a better opportunity."

"Anyway, how was your interview?"

"Nigel baby, your mamma got tha job!"

"That's what's up."

"I'm so excited about it. Makes me feel good, ya know."

"I know. You deserve it."

"Thank you, baby."

"Have you told Victoria?"

"Naw, you know she don't want to have nothing to do with me."

"Ma, on the real, can you blame her?"

"What's that supposed to mean?"

"I know what you've been doing. It's all around town. My friends know too, and they tell me about it."

"How do they know?"

"They mamas be seeing it all on social media. You ain't exactly quiet with it."

"Just stay in your place."

"A'ight Ma, but you know you wrong."

"You sound as if you checkin' for the same helfa that took you from your father."

"I ain't checkin' for her, but she has apologized, and she is your sister."

"Let me worry about all that, and as for her apology…she's got ten years of apologizing to do."

"Whateva Ma. I'm going to do my homework."

Niriya quickly realized she was losing her hold over Nigel concerning Victoria. Her schemes were pushing the one person she loved most into the arms of the person she hated the most. She had some life decisions to make. Meanwhile, Victoria was cooking dinner for her and Raymond.

About three hours later, he walked into the house and began kissing his wife.

"Hey, baby," he said.

"Hey," Victoria responded coldly being that she slaved over dinner, and now it's three hours cold.

"What's wrong?" he asked.

"Nothing. Why are you home so late?" she asked wanting to argue but remembering what God said.

"I've got something to tell you," Raymond said.

"What now?" Victoria said not being able to help herself.

"Can we sit over dinner and talk about it?"

"I guess."

"I know I'm late and I'm sorry and I ain't even trying to argue but I am going to need your full attention for what I'm about to tell you."

"I'm fine…just got a lot on my mind, but you have my full attention," she said as they both sat down for dinner.

"I couldn't really focus on work after our argument this morning, and that's how it's been for a while now. It's like I don't have any peace. I go to a job that doesn't satisfy me, dealing with people who want you to perform miracles with unrealistic budgets and throwing around heavy demands but ain't worth the print the money is painted on. Then, I have to come home to more unrest, fighting with you, dealing with Niriya's foolishness, and all the other crap. Now, it has shown up in my work. Mr. Balstic has taken me off the huge account for Dolan Productions. I have some time off, but honestly, I don't think I have a job anymore. In no uncertain terms, he expects for me to be back on my game when I return," he said awaiting his wife's response. Victoria had a long pause and started thinking to herself, "Lord, is this a test! You said not to argue, and this is what You bring me. Are You serious?" Then Victoria busted out laughing. "This is funny to you?" Raymond asked becoming a little ticked off at his wife's response.

After she calmed down from laughing, she said, "No, it's not funny, but I have to laugh because this is ridiculous, and I have to laugh to keep from saying stuff."

"Like what?"

"This is crazy."

"I can't talk to you."

"Raymond, sit down and chill out. What else do you have to say?"

"Do you even want to hear it?"

"Go ahead. I'm cool."

"I saw you calling but the reason I didn't answer my phone is because I went to the beach. I just sat there all afternoon, thinking about what I was going to say to you, how I would tell you, how you were going to take it, what I needed to do, etc. I came to the realization that I don't know what I'm doing with my life. I seem to be messing it up day by day. I need God to help me in the worst kind of way."

"You and me both."

"I know, right."

"Humph."

"Anyway, as I was sitting on the beach thinking about things, I was watching families spend time together, children playing and watching the water."

"Hmmm…interesting."

"Yeah, so anyway, nothing was lifting me up until I watched the water one last time."

"What happened?"

"A little girl was writing in the sand, and when the water washed up on the shore, it wiped away what the little girl wrote. It caught my attention, and the Lord began to speak to me."

"What'd he say?"

"First, I received a revelation. I realized that whatever we write into our lives (what doesn't belong), God can wash it away no matter how many times you write it, He can cleanse us."

"That's good."

"Yeah, God is so good, and it took that for me to see what I need to do."

"And what's that?"

"I'm going to turn in my resignation and start my own company."

"Really!"

"Yes."

"Yay! Oh, baby, I'm so proud of you! What can I do to help?"

"Start your dream."

"Not right now."

"Why? What are you scared of?"

"I don't know."

"You have put this off for years. It's time."

"Is it really?"

"Yes, Victoria, it is time. Another thing that God showed me is that one of the reasons for all the arguments is because neither one of us is satisfied where we are anymore."

"True."

"Then do something about it."

"I don't know, Raymond."

"You've got to do it. Could it be possible that you are holding up your own blessing?" Raymond asked her placing his hand on her belly.

"Anything's possible," Victoria answered welling up with tears in her eyes and placing her hands on top of his.

"It's time for you to become the interior decorator that you've always wanted to be."

Victoria paused for the loss of words. Then Raymond said, "You are so good at it. Come to think of it, you lost the passion for it after Nigel was born. You stopped working in the field altogether after they moved."

"I couldn't go on following that. I didn't have a right to. There was no way God would bless me behind what I did. And I didn't expect Him to."

"It's time you let go of the guilt. It has been over two years since you came clean. I have forgiven you; God has forgiven you, and even Nigel has forgiven you."

"How do you know that?"

"Come on, Victoria, I see how well you and Nigel get along now. I even found the poem he wrote you a while back."

"Why didn't you ever say anything?"

"It wasn't for me to say anything. When you all were ready to let me know, then that would have been fine. Ria, it's time for you to forgive yourself."

"I know."

"Can I ask you something?"

"Yeah."

"Is that why you don't stand up to Niriya…because of the guilt?"

"Raymond, I don't know. I guess that has something to do with it, but our problems go much deeper than that."

"Why won't you tell me what happened between y'all?"

"I'm just not ready yet."

"Whenever you are ready, I'll be waiting."

"Thank you for understanding."

"Baby, I want you to know I love you."

"Let me say something that's been on my heart to say for a long time concerning Niriya, and maybe this will help some."

"Okay."

"I hear you love me, and I know you do, but what you don't seem to understand is that my worst enemy has a son with my one true love, my husband, you Raymond. Do you know how that makes me feel? Like, less than a woman; here it is I can't give my husband a baby. On top of that, I lowered myself to allow your sperm to impregnate my own sister and all because I'm barren. Now, I have a nephew, who is your son, by my sister, and if we are ever to have a child, that would be his brother-cousin. Man, we sound like something off the discovery channel." Raymond busted out laughing, and Victoria said, "It ain't funny."

"I'm sorry, baby. You are right," Raymond said and started laughing again, hysterically.

"I don't see what's so funny."

"It's the way you said it. I'm sorry…continue."

"I'm pouring out my heart, and you are in tears laughing."

"I don't think it's funny. I'm just laughing at your discovery channel statement."

"Raymond! Ugh, forget it."

"No, no, come here, baby," Raymond said as he wrapped himself around Victoria from the back.

"Uh, uh, I don't want to hear nothing you have to say."

"Come on, sweetness, I'm sorry. Look, I didn't see it that way, but the fact is, we can't change what's already happened. Nigel is here, and Niriya will forever be a part of our lives, and we will have to make the best of it. But, I want you to know that you are all the woman I need. I would have been happy if we had waited on God for our child. That is why you have to talk to me because I won't know how you feel if you don't tell me how you feelin'."

"I should have waited on God."

"We both should have waited but it's okay. God will work it out. I love you, cupcake."

"I love you too, Ray."

Raymond started kissing his wife on the neck, and it felt so good to her. It even felt better because she had been holding that in for a long time. She leaned back into his arms and grew limp. He swept her off her feet and carried her upstairs. Once they were in the bedroom, he laid her on the bed and got to it. I wouldn't even allow Niriya to come and ruin this moment for them. I occupied her time with something else. One thing about Niriya, she had too much time on her hands, and when you have too much time on your hands, you begin to affect other people's lives and not for the good either. Now her time is engaged, entertaining other things. I couldn't let her spoil this; too much is on the line.

Do you want to know why sex is so powerful after an argument? It is because there is a release of oneself. Your guard is down. The argument happened because the guard was up, no one willing to compromise. One is no longer being selfish but is giving from their soul, and that, my friend, is the power of forgiveness. Satan no longer has power over the marriage, the couple, their home, nor the situation…at that point, love and forgiveness have taken over. There's a breaking and destruction of a devil devised plan. The couple wants to prove that they didn't mean what they said or did. The power of love and forgiveness destroys and obliterates the walls built to keep the couple separate. Satan can't, nor does he understand love, and he can't be in the midst of it.

Raymond and Victoria slept through the night. Believe Me, when I say they made up for all the months they didn't "know" each other…in one night. They didn't even get up the next morning. They slept well into the afternoon. Around two o'clock, Raymond got up and packed their suitcases for a week's vacation. He called Nigel before he left and asked him if there was anything he needed or wanted…taking care of his responsibilities. Nigel understood and told his dad to go ahead, and he would see him when they got back. After making all the arrangements, packing up the car, and getting ready, he woke up Victoria, who was calling home the hogs.

"Hey sweetness, wake up," Raymond said.

"Good morning, love," Victoria said with a smile on her face.

"It's time to get up," Raymond said.

"What time is it?" she asked.

"Three-thirty in the afternoon," he said.

"Are you serious?"

"Yep, you were snoring hard too."

"Shut up! Like you don't snore."

"I don't."

"Whateva, Ray."

"Come on and get up. I have some plans for us."

"What are we doing?"

"Just get up and get a shower, and I'll explain all that later."

Victoria got up and prepared herself for the day. Raymond was excited about spending time with Victoria. As they were getting ready to leave, pulling out of the driveway, Joshua pulled up in the driveway with a female in his car. All of them got out of their vehicles, and to Raymond and Victoria's disbelief, Leigha stepped out of Joshua's car.

"Leigha, what is going on?" Victoria said.

"Can we go in the house?" Leigha said.

Full of Surprises

After they entered the house, it was pin-drop quiet. Joshua and Leigha starred at their friends while Raymond wondered what was going on with his friend Joshua and Victoria was just as confused. Raymond broke the silence with a direct question, "Man, what is this about?"

"We got something to ask you guys," Joshua said.

"What is it?" Victoria asked with anticipation.

"We wanted to know if y'all will be witnesses at our wedding," Joshua asked.

"What!" both of them said at the same time.

"When did this happen?" Victoria asked.

"We've been dating for the last two years," Leigha said.

"Why the secrecy Joshua? I didn't even know that you knew Leigha. You usually tell me everything," Raymond said.

"Man, we didn't know where this was going. Once she found out I was saved, she shot me down for months, but I knew she was to be my wife. She finally gave in, and we were going strong for a while. Then we broke for a while," Joshua said.

"Why did y'all break up?" Raymond asked.

"He wouldn't marry me because I hadn't given my life to Christ," Leigha said.

"Wow!" Raymond responded.

"I told you he was serious about this thang," Victoria said laughing.

"I know right," Leigha responded.

"So, what is the difference now?" Raymond asked.

"I got saved two weeks ago," Leigha said.

"Oh my God! Congratulations! Why did I have to wait to find that out?" Victoria asked.

"Girl, you know you have too much going on, and that's why we never said anything," Leigha said.

"You can say that again," Victoria said.

"Did you just get saved to be with Joshua?" Raymond asked, putting a damper on things.

"Ray, man, you are out of line. This is my future wife you're talking to," Joshua said, grabbing ahold of Leigha's hand and looking into her eyes.

"Man, I'm sorry, but you know I'm protective of you. You're like my lil brother," Raymond said.

"I know, man, but be cool. She's been going to church with me for over a year now," Joshua said.

"So that's where you've been," Victoria said.

"Yep, I did good hiding it from you. I didn't know if I could pull it off," Leigha said.

"Y'all did good hiding it from everybody," Raymond said.

"Raymond, to answer your question, I did not get saved for Joshua nor to get married to him. I got saved because Jesus drew me," Leigha said.

"I gotta check because you know you off tha hook," Raymond said.

"So, when is the wedding?" Victoria asked.

"Tomorrow," Joshua said.

"Tomorrow?" Raymond said.

"Yes, we are going to the church and having a small ceremony," Joshua said.

"Very small," Leigha said.

"Why so small and so quick?" Victoria asked.

"Neither one of us want a big wedding, we'd rather save our money for a house and traveling, plus we've waited long enough. On top of that, you know work got me humpin', so it has to be quick," Joshua said.

"Can you guys be there?" Leigha asked.

Victoria looked at Raymond to see what he was going to say. He nodded his head and said, "Yes, we will be there. We were about to leave, but I'll hold off till tomorrow."

"Where we're y'all going?" Joshua asked.

"I had some surprises for my wife, so I'd rather not say," Raymond said.

"How about tomorrow we all go out of town after the wedding?" Joshua asked.

"Wait a minute now; I've been waiting years for a piece, and you ain't goin' to jip me of mines. No offense, girl," Leigha said and everyone started laughing.

"None taken," Victoria responded.

"Ah, don't worry, you will get yours. Believe that. I ain't been saved all my life," Joshua said.

"Hmph…can't wait," Leigha said.

"Leigha, let me holla at you over here for a minute," Victoria said.

"Sure, what's up?" Leigha asked.

"If y'all been together for so long, what was up with ol' dude a while back?" Victoria asked.

"That was when we broke up, and I was so mad at him, one because he wasn't giving it up and two because he didn't want to get married as long as I was a "heathen," Leigha said laughing.

"I know you weren't trippin' because he wouldn't have sex with you," Victoria said.

"Yes, I was. Girl, you know me, and he wasn't playin'. He told me that he's been waiting this long; he can continue to wait. It didn't bother him at all," Leigha said.

"I told you how he was, and you didn't believe me," Victoria said.

"I'll let you in on another little secret," she said.

"What now, Leigha?" said Victoria.

"That wasn't the first time that we met when we were having brunch that day. By that time, we had already been dating a couple of weeks," Leigha said.

"Are you serious? When did y'all meet?" Victoria asked.

"Do you remember when you took me to Raymond's office for the Christmas party?" Leigha asked.

"Yeah," Victoria responded.

"That's when we met, and that day we had brunch; he wanted to see me, so he dropped by," Leigha said.

"But I don't understand all the secrecy. Why didn't you feel like you could tell me? I mean, it's not like we would have focused on y'all. We had enough that we were dealing with on our own," Victoria asked.

"I know, but we just didn't want to tell anybody," Leigha said.

"I guess Leigha, but I am happy for y'all," Victoria said.

The next day, Raymond and Victoria attended the wedding of their friends. It was nice and simple. They were ecstatic to be at the wedding of their best friends, Joshua and Leigha Stokes. They decided to go ahead and go on vacation together at the white sands of Destin, FL. As a gift to the newlyweds, he funded their vacation. They just had to pay for food and whatever else they wanted to do. Their rooms were on different floors (wink, wink). Neither of them wanted disturbances, especially Leigha. I won't get into their wild and intimate nights. It would be too graphic for some of your ears, and some of you that are religious wouldn't be able to handle it as if you don't know what married people do. You would promise that it is flesh talking instead of Me.

The morning after, they got together for breakfast and made plans for the day. They chose to do some things together and some things apart. Raymond used this time to minister the love to his wife that he deprived her of all those years. Victoria is relieved from stress, enjoying her time with her husband and her best friend. She is having the best of times. It's been a long time since she has felt like this. Joshua and Leigha are glowing, and Raymond and Victoria made sure that they let them know that too.

"Man Joshua, are you going to cheese any harder? You've been smiling all morning," said Raymond.

"It just feels good to do things the right way. You can enjoy it better, and the Lawd knows I enjoyed last night with my baby," Joshua said.

"I was scared at first because I didn't know what to expect, but God didn't let me down. He knew I needed a man that could "help a sista out" and give me what I need," Leigha said. They all laughed.

"Boy, the Lord sure has his work cut out for Him because you are a piece of work. You sure you saved," Raymond said joking. He and Leigha had that brother-sister report.

"Shut up, Raymond!" Leigha yelled and smiled.

"Don't play, girl. You know you off the hook," Raymond said.

"Come on, baby, you know he's telling the truth," said Joshua backing up his friend.

"Awh, you gone take his side? I'd be careful with that if I were you," said Leigha.

"What you gone do?" Joshua inquired.

"You'll see," Leigha said.

"Hurt me, baby!" Joshua said.

"Uhm, Ray baby, I think it's time for us to go," Victoria said.

"You know what I'm sayin," Raymond said.

"Yeah, y'all might have to do that because I see right now I'm going to have to check her," Joshua said, picking up his new wife and carrying her over his shoulder. Leigha is laughing and embarrassed.

Leigha looked back and waved, then yelled, "Whew! Tha lawd know what I need!"

The newlyweds went off happy and in love while Raymond and Victoria went off holding hands, walking on the sparkling, glistening sands of the island, talking about good stuff. They left their problems back at home. They didn't talk about Niriya, Nigel, the promised son, or the arguing they had been doing. They put out a spiritual cease and desist on all their issues and enjoyed one another's company instead.

After walking on the secluded beach and playing in the beautiful teal bluish-green water, they found a spot hidden from other people. They talked some more while lying under the umbrella they set up.

"I love that swimsuit on you. The colors bring out the caramel color of your skin."

"Thank you," Victoria said grinning from ear to ear as if she had heard this for the first time.

"Even now, the sunlight shining through the water is in the perfect spot to capture the sparkle in your eyes."

"Wow! I got a sparkle! Let me see," Victoria said.

"Leave it to you to turn a sentimental moment into a comedy session."

"Oh, Ray baby, don't be like that. You are just as sexy as me."

"As you, huh?"

"Hey, I gotta be me."

"What's that?" Ray asked so he could get her to roll over and look in the opposite direction.

"What's what? I don't see anything."

"Oh, my bad cupcake."

"Cupcake? Oh, you only call me that when you..."

"Then you know what I want."

"And what's that?"

"Don't play. You know what time it is."

"Boy, what are you doing!"

"What do you mean?"

"My gawd! You can't put your hand there. Somebody is going to see us."

"So! Let 'em watch but I'll put this towel over you if that will make you feel more comfortable."

"And how are you going to explain the arrest record to Pastor?"

"Scaredy cat."

"Whateva. I ain't scared. I'm just…" Victoria tried to say but let out a moan instead.

"Come here," Raymond said as he had her sit on top of him with her wrap covering them. She said, "I can't believe we are doing this." He said, "Ain't nobody paying us any attention. This part of the beach is secluded, and if anyone is out here, they are probably doing the same thing, so relax and enjoy." She was nervous and he relished in the moment.

Joshua and Leigha weren't that far away doing the same thing. See, that's what marriage is all about. It's not just work, but it's an enjoyment of one another. It's not all bad, but there are some good times too. Married couples tend to do the same thing as the media, exploiting the bad things and hardly reporting the good, which is one of the reasons why marriages fail. The couples esteem one higher than the other, and unfortunately, it's the bad that's esteemed the highest. Yes, marriage isn't a fairy-tale, but it's not a "chain-gang" either. While I'm here, let Me dispute this idea that marriage is a prison. It's anything but that. Marriage is freedom, freedom to be all you are vicariously through your spouse.

ATTENTION MARRIED COUPLES!!! STOP LIVING AS TWO, SEPARATE. I DIDN'T ORDAIN MARRIAGE FOR SEPARATION OR TO DIVIDE. I ORDAINED IT TO COME TOGETHER, BE IN UNITY. YOU BECOME WHOLE, AS ONE. AS LONG AS YOU LIVE AS TWO, YOU WILL NEVER FUNCTION AS ONE. It's like a band or an orchestra. To have harmony, the instruments must be tuned up first and follow the same sheet of music. It doesn't take long for an instrument to tune up. It only takes a couple of seconds (unless something is wrong, then it takes longer, in which case you have to take it to the shop to get it fixed).

Take the time to tune up your marriage daily, just like an instrument must be tuned up before it is played. When you do that, you will be able to pick up when something is out of tune a whole lot easier and handle it before it gets worse. If both the husband and wife follow and play the same sheet of music, it will work. However, if there comes a time you find that the tuning isn't working, take it to the shop (counseling) to get it fixed. When attending counseling, it doesn't work if you don't work it, nor does it work if you do not heed the therapist's guidance. When fine-tuning your marriage, make sure you're not pointing the finger and blaming the other person. Tuning starts with you first, not your spouse. As soon as you take the focus off them and look inward, that's when you will find the healing mechanism.

♦♦♦♦♦♦♦♦   Back to their Story   ♦♦♦♦♦♦♦♦

As the week went on, Raymond and Victoria fell more deeply in love, and they renewed their vows on the island and made promises to each other. Joshua and Leigha were there to support them as friends do. They knew all that Raymond and Victoria had been through over the past years. Raymond had all this planned. He made a promise to Me that he wouldn't give his wife a reason to have to scheme and feel like she is all alone and less than a woman. He vowed to love his wife as himself (Eph 5:28) and that he would not be bitter towards her (Col 3:19). He did not let Victoria know what he promised to Me concerning her. I had to deal with him harshly because I never intend for a wife to feel less than loved to the point she feels like she has to resort to all-time lows to get the love that is due to her from the husband that promised to love her. That wasn't My intention, it never has been. He is making good on his vow. He paid it immediately and continues to do so.

When they got home, Victoria nixed all her plans to destroy Niriya. She vowed to Me that she would love her sister and do everything in her power to make it right, but she also decided that she wasn't going to take any more off her either. I dealt with her harshly, as well. I told her it was time to come clean to Raymond. He needs to know the whole truth. If she wants the issues to get better, she has to clear the air. I spoke with her about how she's supposed to make her husband feel. Husbands should feel honored and respected. They shouldn't have to protect themselves from lies the wives tell. For them, that's betrayal. A husband should always be able to trust his wife (Pro 31:11). Victoria had Raymond call Nigel to tell him to come over because she bought him something that she knew he would love. Raymond set it up for him before he arrived.

"Hey Nigel," Victoria said and greeted him with a hug.

"Hi Victoria," Nigel said.

"Hey, son," Raymond said.

"Wuz up pops," Nigel said.

"Boy, get over here and give your father a hug. Stop trying to be macho," Raymond said and smiled. Nigel walked over to his dad laughing.

"Y'all are a trip," Victoria said.

"Man, I missed y'all," Nigel said.

"We missed you too," Raymond said.

"What did you do while we were gone?" Victoria asked.

"Nothing much. I went to school. Momma's been working," Nigel said.

"I'm glad she got that job," Victoria said.

"Me too," he said.

"That's good," Raymond said.

"Momma didn't have anyone to share it with, and she was kinda down about it. She really wanted to share it with you, but you know how she is," Nigel said.

"I will talk to her but I will act surprised when she tells me," Victoria said, and Raymond looked at his wife in shock because he wasn't sure where she was going with this.

"I know she'll like that, but you know she probably will try to play like she ain't pressed by it," Nigel said.

"I know my sister, in and out. Don't you worry. I got this," Victoria said and Raymond was on pins and needles.

"Cool," Nigel said.

"Come on, your dad, and I want to show you something," Victoria said.

"What is it? Y'all got me something?" Nigel asked becoming excited.

"Wait and see," his father said. When they walked into the den, Nigel's eyes got big, and a grin was slapped widely across his face.

"Awh, man! Now, this is what's up!" Nigel exclaimed.

"Do you like it?" his father asked him.

"That's mine?" Nigel asked.

"Yes," Victoria answered.

"Cool! I always wanted a keyboard, and y'all got tha whole shebang, the stand, bench, microphone, different sheet music, and sound system," Nigel said.

"We knew you liked music, and you have talent, so when Victoria saw it, she thought about you and had to get it," his father said.

"You are welcome any time to come over and practice on it," Victoria said.

"Can I play it now?" he asked.

"Of course," his father answered.

"While y'all do this, I'm going over to talk to Niriya," Victoria said.

"Alright, sweetness," her husband said.

Nigel didn't hear what Victoria said because he was already playing the keyboard and figuring everything out. His father watched on to see his son expressing excitement doing something he loved.

Victoria went next door to talk to her sister. "Who is it?" Niriya answered.

"It's Victoria," she answered.

Niriya opened the door with an insult, "Well, well, well, if it ain't the tramp who's back from her whore trip."

It took everything within Victoria not to knock her head right off her shoulders and asked, "Can I come in? We need to talk."

"Only for a minute; I really don't have nothing to say to you," her sister said.

"That's fine," Victoria answered as she walked into the house.

"So, what is this about?" Niriya asked getting straight to the point.

"I wanted to say, I'm sorry. I'm sorry for everything I've ever done to you to make you mad at me. I'm sorry for making you feel like you didn't belong or less than me. I'm sorry for moving you away as if you were a nobody and didn't matter. I'm sorry for pretending to be something I wasn't growing up and letting you take the heat for everything. I caused you a lot of pain. I caused you a lot of hurt, and I didn't help you have a better life. I may not have been the source of all your problems, but I was a good chunk of it. Niriya, you are my sister, and I love you despite what you may believe," Victoria said.

"Why did you let me take the fall? Why didn't you stand up to mother? Why did you turn your back on me? You knew I longed for mother's approval and her love, and you made her believe that I was the bad one," Niriya said while trying to hold back tears but they fell just as quickly.

"I know, and I'm sorry," Victoria said.

"But why?" Niriya asked again.

"I don't know why. You knew how mother was, and I just couldn't do it at the time. I was scared," Victoria said.

Niriya dried up her tears and became angry, "If you truly came over here to apologize, then you are going to have to better than that. You got me put out of the house. You watched and did nothing. How do I forgive that?"

"Honestly, I thought we were over this hump," she said.

"Victoria, how could you possibly think that? Do you not realize the damage you did?" her sister asked.

"When I apologized about it before, we became the best of friends. That's why I felt comfortable asking you to be a surrogate mother for me," Victoria explained.

"I played you *just* like you played me. And I patiently waited for the perfect opportunity to repay you for everything you did to me and what you didn't do *for* me. Pretending to accept your apology was just the beginning. Don't you believe for one second that I hadn't been plotting to get back at you for the pain you caused me. I waited for a long time. Then when you asked me to be a surrogate mom for you, BINGO, the door flew wide open. I *never* had plans on giving you Nigel. I absolutely enjoyed the look in your eyes every time I walked past you with my belly growing every day. The sheer joy for me was knowing I could give your husband what you neva could. And I still don't feel bad about it. Yeah…dats right; look at you; you're scared now. Cry the tears I've cried for years. Feel my pain, FEEL – MY – WRATH!" Niriya yelled as she pointed a butcher knife at Victoria's throat, backing her up on the kitchen wall.

"I did not know how deep your hatred was for me until now. I don't know what else to say, Niriya. I don't even know what else to do," Victoria cried but spoke softly and cautiously as to not move the knife that was at her throat.

"Niriya, what are you doing!" Raymond came through the door and grabbed her by the wrist, barely nicking his wife's throat with the knife.

"Niriya, I'm sorry. I didn't know. I didn't know," Victoria said as she walked out of the house holding her neck that a blood on it.

Raymond let Niriya's arms go and walked out behind Victoria. He knew his wife going to talk to her sister wasn't going to be a good thing, which is why he went to check on her. Niriya stood there in the kitchen, leaning forward on the kitchen table in disbelief and shock. She thought following through on the many violent ideations she's had over the years would feel good but she found out that it didn't. She didn't realize she hated her sister that much. It opened her eyes and she began to pack her things to leave that night. She didn't say goodbye to her son, her sister, or Raymond.

Raymond followed hard after Victoria asking her what had happened.

"Raymond, just leave it alone!"

He grabbed her by the arm and took her upstairs so Nigel couldn't hear.

"Let me go, Raymond!"

"No! Not until you tell me what is going on?"

"It's nothing."

"I ain't fazed by your tears. You are going to tell me what happened, and you are going to tell me now!"

"Why can't you just leave this between my sister and me?"

"You want to know why? Because I just walked in on Niriya holding a knife to *my* wife's neck! That's why? So, start talking."

"I went over to apologize for everything that I've done to her."

"God! What happened to y'all as kids?"

"When we moved out of the hood into the house down the street, mother changed. Daddy made the money, but mother ran the house and caused havoc if daddy tried to be the man of the house. Mother was very demanding, and things were going to be done her way. When she got around all those sidity folk, she'd put on heirs. We had to be perfect. She didn't want people to know where we came from. Daddy didn't like it. They were arguing all the time, especially about us girls. There was a time when they split up for months. They didn't talk to each other, nothing. Daddy would come to see us at school and call us. Eventually, they got back together. We really wanted to go live with him because living with momma was horrible. Niriya wanted desperately to win over momma's affections. I wanted her to love me too, and I don't have a doubt that she did love us, but I had a love-fear for mother. She could be sweet at times, and at other times she could be a monster."

"Did she abuse y'all?" Raymond asked.

"Physically, no, at least not anything out of the norm, but she totally damaged us emotionally and mentally. There was something big that happened, though, that split my sister and me —I guess, forever. We used to be so close, but our relationship could not withstand the power of the fear of mother."

"Victoria, that's deep."

"Oh, don't get ahead of me. There is more shoveling to do."

Raymond let out a little giggle when Victoria said that and said, "Alright baby, what big thing happened?"

"When I was seventeen, a junior in high school, I became pregnant by Niriya's boyfriend."

"What! Did he rape you?"

"No, he didn't rape me. We were at a party one night, and we were all getting high."

"You, high?"

"Don't act like you didn't know because we used to do it when we started dating senior year."

"Yeah, you right. I forgot about that."

"How convenient. You know how you used to be."

"But I've changed."

"Yes, you did, and I love you for it. Anyway, we're getting off track. Well, Niriya wasn't at the party. Mother said she was too young to go, and mother didn't know that Niriya was dating a junior. See, she was only a freshman.

Anyway, we were all having a good time at the party, and someone came up with the bright idea to play spin the bottle. So, you can only guess what happened next."

"The bottle landed on you two."

"Exactly. He spent the bottle, and it landed on me. We both looked at each other and tried to get out of it, but they wouldn't budge. They said that if we didn't do it, they would tell Niriya that we did. Needless to say, we went into the bedroom. We contemplated for a long time, but then everyone started knocking on the door, talking about hurry up. Talk about blowin' a high."

"You ain't lyin'."

"Anyway, we went ahead and kissed. But I can't lie, we both started to enjoy it, and that's where everything started. After we came out when our seven minutes were up, they stopped playing the game, and everybody was matched up gettin' their groove on, so we left and went to his house. We felt guilty at first, but our lust overrode any guilt we had. Nobody knew but him and me. We never said anything to anybody, and especially not to Niriya. Consequently, though, it hit the fan because I became pregnant. I told him about it, and he freaked."

"How did Niriya find out?"

"Raymond, that's still a mystery because I didn't tell her and I'm sure he didn't because they kept dating after we slept together. I guess he talked to somebody because I didn't tell a soul, not even Leigha. But whoever he told must have spread it around because all I know is one day she came home from school and punched me in my face."

"Which was well deserved."

"I guess. We only slept together that one time."

"Don't get mad with me, Victoria. One time or not, I'd probably have punched you too."

"Whateva! Do you want me to finish or not?"

"Aye, do you."

"We started fighting right there in the house. Daddy broke up the fight and wondered what we were fighting about, but neither one of us said anything. He didn't understand it and neither did I. She didn't rat me out, which was a surprise. Mother was furious with Niriya and comforted me. I didn't speak up, nor did I tell the truth."

"Victoria, what happened with the baby?"

"While I was deciding on what to do, because I knew I couldn't have this baby, mother would kill me; about three months into the pregnancy, I had a miscarriage. The father of the baby took me to the emergency room at the community hospital, and when I signed in, I signed in under Niriya's name."

"Dawg Victoria, I didn't know you could be so scandalous. That's cold."

"I know. I try not to be like that."

"What happened after that?"

"Everything had cooled down for a while until the medical bill came to the house."

"I was wondering how a seventeen-year-old was going to pull that off."

"I didn't think that far ahead, hence the butt-whoopin' that was coming up next. When mother read over everything, she hit the fan. You know how we say that we can't stand in God's wrath; well, apparently, He hadn't met mothers. Her wrath was fierce, and you know who caught it all?"

"Niriya."

"Yep, because her name was on the bill. She tried to tell mother that it wasn't her but she wasn't trying to hear it. Even daddy was disappointed in her, which really killed her inside."

"No doubt."

"She caught it, and it changed the mood in our house forever. Daddy finally came around though, but mother never forgot it. After that, Niriya was "hell on wheels.""

"No wonder that girl can't stand you."

"Do you see why I wouldn't stand up to her? One, I didn't want her to say anything to you, so I was willing to take anything she dished out. Two, I deserved it after all I put her through."

"You never apologized?"

"I did. Mother kicked her out the house a year later for something completely different. I found her, and we sat down and talked about everything, and I told her I was sorry. We made amends, or so I thought."

"What do you mean by that?"

"We became close after that. I even convinced mother to let her back in the house so she could focus on school. Subsequently, that was all a part of Niriya's plan to get back at me."

"Plan?"

"Yes, when I was just over there, she was saying that it was all a part of her plan. She waited for the right opportunity to get me back, and she saw it when we asked her to be the surrogate. It was never her intention to give me Nigel. I told her in confidence (when I thought her love for me was genuine) that when I had the miscarriage, the doctor told me that I would never be able to get pregnant again because apparently, my insides were botched up. She used that every chance she got and mocked me."

"Wa…wait a minute," Raymond said confused, then continued, "What you mean you can't have kids?"

"Ray…"

"Naw, Ray nothin'! You mean to tell me after all this time, you knew you couldn't have kids and didn't tell me!" Victoria tried to respond, but he wasn't having it. He sat down on the bed in shock. Then he said, "You know what, Victoria, you deserve what you got. What you did to her was cold. You are conniving, and I'm done. That was the last straw. I have forgiven you for the most horrible things, but you can't keep droppin' bombs and expect for me to keep being cool about it. You have violated my trust way too many times. How many blows do you expect me to take?"

"Don't say that. I've stayed with you during your mistakes, so why is it any different when it's your turn to stay through mine?"

"Oh, here we go! I like how you bring up what you said you forgave me for just to justify your ish."

"But it has merit. You keep treating me like trash because of what I did, but at least I admitted to it nor did you have find out through someone else. And yes, that was a dig at you."

"And you think that helps you get out of this?"

"No, but I want to remind you that your slate ain't squeaky clean either and you're not just going to keep throwing stuff in my face as if you haven't done ish to hurt me. Now, do you want me to finish telling you what happened or not?"

"Gone head."

"I promise it will all make sense. If you still want to leave after hearing it, then I won't fight it."

"Fine but you don't deserve it."

"Raymond, don't you think I know that, but I tried to right my wrongs. Look, I told mother that it was me instead of Niriya. I told her everything that happened, every gory detail, but mother wouldn't believe it. She said that Niriya shouldn't have me lying for her to get back in the house. I told daddy too, and he believed me and was disappointed in me too, but he loved me despite it all. He didn't make me feel bad and dirty."

"What did your mom have against Niriya? Sounds like she was heartless towards her."

"I don't know what that was all about, but I do know her and daddy fell out about it all the time. Daddy didn't play around when it came to his daughters. He didn't care who you were or where you came from and mother was not an exception."

"Sounds like more family secrets."

"Yes, but I'm not even trying to dig. Let it be what it be.

"But you had to expect she was going to retaliate."

"I tried to make it right, Raymond."

"Okay, but even you said it yourself that y'all was never the same after all that. You got off easy if you ask me."

"See, this is why I didn't want to tell you because you are judging me and acting as if I should be punished for life. You're worse than everybody else. You act as if *your* closet is clean. I've paid the price. I'm forty-five with the curse of not being able to bear a child, a husband that looks at me differently, a nephew that is my husband and sister's son, and a jacked-up relationship with my sister. I've paid it twice over. I've paid a lot longer than what she endured."

"I'm going to tell you the truth, no matter how it makes you feel. You can't deny that you played a huge role in messing up her life. I don't have sympathy for you, and you know why?"

"Oh, gee! Please Raymond, please tell me why oh great one!"

"See. You see that right there. You know what? Never mind. I don't feel sorry for you because you didn't think about me or my feelings when you hid this and didn't even tell me that you couldn't have a baby. Here I believed that one day we would have a house full of children, and you knew the whole time that you couldn't have kids."

"Raymond, two weeks after we got married, during altar call at church, what did the pastor say?"

"He said that God was going to touch your womb and bless us with a son."

"Did you believe it then?"

"Of course, but it would have helped if you would have told me the truth."

"Helped you do what? Doubt what God was saying?"

"No, but at least I would have known what I was up against."

"Look, I'm sorry for not telling you."

"Man, Victoria…"

"I knew I never should have told you. I knew you weren't going to be able to handle it, and it's okay."

"What do you mean by that?"

"Just what I said."

"I know you Victoria, and I know there is a meaning behind what you just said."

"Raymond, really, nothing behind it. I'm good."

Victoria left the room. There was something behind what she said, but he wouldn't find out until later. She checked on Nigel, and he was still downstairs playing on his keyboard. He was really into it too. Victoria knew he'd love it. Raymond sat up in the bedroom, puzzled by what Victoria had just told him. He didn't know his wife could be so conniving. He wondered if she had done something else in their marriage that he didn't know about. He laid back on his bed, thinking about all that was said. He fell into a deep sleep, and that's when Victoria's "behind the meaning" went into action. She packed her clothes and left. I tell you; this child is always running from her problems. Little does she know; I'm going to turn her right around. She won't get far.

Nigel didn't even notice she had left the house. He went up to his room and went to sleep after hours upon hours of playing the keyboard. He's quite good. He will do something with it someday.

Around 1:00 am Raymond, woke up to find that his wife was not at home. "I knew there was something behind what that girl said," he thought to himself. Then I said to him, "You vowed to Me you would love her. You said, and I quote, "I will love my wife, and I won't give her a reason to have to scheme and feel like she is all alone and less than a woman. I will love her as myself, and I won't be bitter towards her." That love isn't based on condition. She already felt bad enough. I didn't punish her like that. She punished herself. When she asked for forgiveness, I gave it to her. When she tried to restore the relationship within her family, I restored her at that moment. Yes, she had to face the consequences, but she turned her life around. You should have been there for her; instead, you condemned her, which is something even I don't do. She told you because she thought she was free to tell you. She thought you would love her enough to receive what she told you without condemning her. Believe Me, if she didn't want to tell you, you wouldn't have known. You were so judgmental. Need I remind you of your past? Need I bring up *your* past sins within your marriage? If I were to take your life right now and you were standing before Me waiting to be judged, what would I show you concerning the life you lived? Don't get so holy now. Don't be so quick to judge, hold grudges and be bitter towards your wife because if I were to flash *your* life before you and in front of her, what would she see and what would you do?"

"Lord, I hear what you are saying, but she never told me that she couldn't have children before we were married. That should have been something that was told to me."

"But neither one of you discussed marriage nor children in its entirety before you got married. Y'all were just so in love and didn't take the time to invest in communicating about what you wanted and what you expected. There were a lot of things y'all should have discussed that you didn't, and you can't blame her for not telling you. You didn't tell her some things either. Did you tell her where your family's money really comes from? Did you tell her what her mother said to you before she died? Did you tell her about Chana while y'all were dating in college? This isn't even what she knows. She's given you chance after chance with what she does know. See, you got some stuff too. So, get off your high horse before you fall off."

After that, Raymond didn't have much to say because he knew I was right, and he wouldn't win. I don't know why my children always try to combat Me with their feelings (which I don't mind), but at the end of the day, truth is what will stand, and your feelings will wither away. I told him to go find his wife.

Victoria forgot that Leigha is married now. She can't just jump up and go visit her girl, mainly because she's married to her husband's best friend. This really put a damper on things. She went to a bar downtown. Victoria made it up in her mind that she would have a drink and get drunk. The devil convinced her that every time she has a little happiness, and just when she thinks everything is going well, something comes along to ruin it. She felt like this was what she was destined for. She completely blocked Me out. I couldn't get to her because her feelings and flesh spoke louder than My spirit. She could hear the devil plain and clear.

When My children get like that, I step back. I try to be there as much as possible, but I have to be wanted. I do not go where I'm not invited. She invited the devil by listening to him and giving in to what he was saying. She feels like he has more validity because he presents the facts to her. What Victoria isn't aware of is that facts can always change, but truth stands, and it stands alone. I have my angels there whenever she is ready to receive Me and hear what I have to say, but while the devil is working on her, I am working on her husband to rescue her. I just need someone to hear Me so they can get through to her. If that happens, then her ear is tender towards My voice.

There Can't Be More!

Raymond was driving all over Jacksonville looking for his wife. He has been over Joshua and Leigha's to see if she was there, but he didn't knock on the door because he didn't see Victoria's car. He went to all her hot spots but to no avail, no Victoria.

"Lord, it's 2:30 in the morning. Where is she at? You told me to go and look for her. Why do You have me out here and then not tell me where she is?"

I answered him, "You are not listening to Me. You are leaning on what you know instead of being in tune with Me. I could have driven you straight there, but you wouldn't listen."

He pulled over and prayed. I showed him the bar she was at and gave him a street name. He knew exactly where the bar was because that was the bar that he went to many years ago when Victoria revealed her secret concerning Nigel. Raymond gave Me an "okay Lord" kind of grin. Twelve minutes later, he pulled up to the bar, and low and behold, there was his wife's car just like I told him. He went in just in time to take the last drink out of her hand and to pull her away from a man that was talking to her.

"What are you doing?" Victoria said barely able to hold up her head.

"I don't think the lady wants to be bothered," said the well-built, wavy hair, light-skinned, muscle man.

"Bruh, you don't want none," Raymond said sternly.

"I paid for that drink. You gone give it back to her," he said.

"Look, I don't need you protecting me. I got this. Plus, I didn't ask you to buy me the drink anyway. Gone 'bout your business," said Victoria with a slurred speech while shaking the same drink that she took back from Raymond. He threw up his hands, walked away, and called her out her name. Raymond drew back his fist to hit the guy, but Victoria stopped him.

"Go home, Raymond!" Victoria said as she signaled for the bartender to make her another drink.

"You are coming with me," Raymond said.

"You ain't my daddy. How did you find me anyway?" she asked.

"God told me," he replied.

"Humph," Victoria sneered.

"Let's go, Ria," her husband demanded. Raymond paid the bartender the money for Victoria's drinks, including the one the other guy paid for. "Ria, how much did you have to drink?"

"Wouldn't you like to know,"

"You know, I've been here before," Raymond told her.

"Ohhh my gaaaawwwwd, what – is – with all the conversation!" she said in a drunken tone.

"I'm going to ignore that. Anyway, I came here when you first told me about Nigel. I was sitting right here when the man Caleb came up and started talking to me. I ordered a Black Russian, and before I could take my first sip, Caleb stepped in and stopped me."

"Yeah. Well, I ain't met no Caleb, no Abraham, no Isaac, nor Jacob either."

"Let's go somewhere else and talk, sweetheart."

"Uhm…No. —bartender! Refill."

Raymond inconspicuously nodded his head no to the bartender and said to Victoria, "We can do this the easy way or the hard way, but either way, you are leaving this bar in the next ten seconds."

"Are you threatening me?"

"One."

"Psh."

"Two."

"I'on know who you think you punkin', but you better ask somebody."

"Three…Four…Five."

"You ain't scaring me."

"Six…Seven."

"Humph."

Raymond stood up and said, "Eight…Nine," as he began to pick her up.

Victoria jumped up and said, "Alright, alright, alright! Let go of me! I can walk."

Raymond grabbed her coat and laughed to himself, watching his wife "step lively" out of the bar like a little kid and about to fall. He told her to leave her car, and they would come back to get it later. They got into his car and began to talk about what happened.

"Look, Ria, I'm sorry for judging you. I should have just listened and supported you better than I did. You were telling me your most deep and intimate secrets, and I threw it in your face. And if you can't share it with me, then who can you share it with?"

"Still with all the talking…anyway, I knew you would not be able to handle it, but I didn't want to hang on to it any longer either. At that point, you could have loved me or left me, and I wouldn't have even cared. I lost the love of my sister and life. Didn't even realize how much she hated me until tonight."

"Are you okay?"

"Am I okay?" Victoria said with a little sarcastic giggle. She continued to say, "No, but I will be. And I'm sorry for not telling you about not being able to have children. You were right. I should have told you."

"Ria, we have to stop having days like this. We had a good time over the past week and our first night back look where we are and what we are doing. I'm sick of days like this. So, from now on, THIS is the last time THIS craziness will happen. We are moving past it."

"I feel you." Victoria tried to continue talking, but something was brewing in her throat. She said, "Pul..pullover! Pullover!" He couldn't stop fast enough. She opened the car door and vomited on the ground. He got out the car and tried to help Victoria as much as possible. After she was finished, he got back in the car and drove home. She didn't want to have any more conversation in fear of vomiting again, but Raymond had jokes.

"Babe, can I say one more thing?"

"What."

"You didn't believe I was going to carry you out there at first, did you?"

"No."

"Shouldn't you know me by now? You know I make good on my threats. I'm not going to lie, though; I was laughing at the way you walked out of the bar. You looked like a lil kid having a temper tantrum."

"Whateva."

They went home and rested from the night's woes, well, at least after Victoria vomited up all that liquor. She was up for a while on the side of the toilet, praying, talking about if I just let her live through this, she'll never do it again—poor child.

They didn't' know what tomorrow was going to bring. Their plans were to sleep in late because, by the time they got home, it was after 2:30 AM. Before they fell asleep, Raymond said to Victoria, "If you are going to have me up at almost three in the morning chasing you around the city, the least you could do is give me some." She just laughed. After laughing, you already know what she did…passed out.

The following morning, around 10:26, Nigel busted into their bedroom and said in a panic, "Ma is gone!"

"What a minute, son…say that again," Raymond replied, woozy.

"Ma's gone!" Nigel repeated.

"What do you mean she's gone?" Raymond said a little more alert, "Ria, wake up."

"Can y'all keep it down, please? And tell me what is going on. Victoria said.

"Get up. Niriya's gone," Raymond reiterated.

"Huh?" Victoria groaned, puzzled and a little woozy with a hangover.

"Dawg gone, what is up with you James women up and leaving! Y'all are some nut-jobs," Raymond said shaking his head.

"Watch yourself," Victoria said getting out of bed.

"I know. My bad, but dawg. Man, it's too early for this crap," Raymond said.

They all walked over to the house. Victoria's hair was all over the place, she put on shades to block the sun as much as possible, and she looked disheveled. When they got there, Raymond asked, "Nigel, what makes you think your mother left. There is nothing out of place or missing?"

"I went to her room to tell her about my new keyboard, and when I did, I found this letter on her bed," Nigel said.

"Let me see…." Dear Nigel, If you are reading this letter, then you've realized I'm gone. Stay with your father. He really loves you. I'll be back, but there are some things I must straighten out. I can't explain it right now, but I will in time. You aren't aware of some of the things going on, and I must straighten it out on my end. Last night, I realized that I need help, and I need it quickly to keep my sanity. Please don't be mad at me and don't blame anyone for this. I have to do this for myself to raise you better. I can't help you if I can't help myself. I'm not gone forever, but I am gone for a time. I love you more than you could ever know, and what I'm doing right now, I'm doing for you. Love, Your Ma." Son, I know you may not see it now, but I know what she is talking about, and she will be back soon," said his father.

Nigel wanted to cry, but his pride wouldn't let him. He was so angry. He couldn't believe this was happening again. First, it was his father, and now it's his mother. All he hoped for was that it wouldn't take another ten years.

Meanwhile, Victoria was in tears because she couldn't help taking some responsibility. She'd hope to someday be reconciled with her sister. I put it in both her and Raymond's hearts not to look for Niriya. I told them to just let her be, and she will return soon.

Six and a half months have rolled by and Niriya has not come back. Victoria has gained an excessive amount of weight. She has been sick for some time. When Raymond took her to the doctor, they found out that she was depressed; she became ill from the stress of her sister's leaving and guilt. She also wondered, if God truly restored her, and if so, then why isn't she pregnant yet. She still feels cursed, barren because of what she did.

Raymond isn't the vain type, but he was turned off by his wife. She wouldn't do anything around the house except sit and eat all day. She fell deeper into depression because she frequently thought about her childhood and how she hurt her sister. Every day that Niriya was gone was another day of not forgiving herself. Raymond watched as his wife swirled deeper and deeper into despair. There was nothing he could do. He had one last trick up his sleeve in hopes it would work. She isn't listening to anyone. Then it seemed like everyone around her was pregnant except her, women at church, women in the neighborhood, and all were having baby showers back-to-back which compounded the depression.

Victoria didn't let that stop her, though. Every week, she went to her sister's house, switched out flowers, and took care of Niriya's home, no matter how sick she got.

"Are you going to put on any clothes or even cook or clean your own house?" Raymond asked.

Victoria didn't say anything and looked at him with her eyes crossed, then continued to watch the soap opera and eat her barbeque potato chips.

"I am sick of this, Victoria! You have done nothing but sit around the house, eat, and get fat. What about me? What about Nigel?"

"What about it?" Victoria said.

"Is that how you are going to answer me?" Raymond asked.

"What do you want me to say?" Victoria answered.

"This is too much, and I can't deal with it."

"Then don't."

"Victoria, I do not understand. You've been in those same pajamas for two days, your hair hasn't been combed since…I don't know when, you haven't cooked for months, and your weight gain is ridiculous!"

"And?"

"And, and…I didn't get married for this. I've had enough of your ups and downs, and this time it's going to give you what you want."

"What does that mean?"

"Get out!"

"Psh…this is my house, and I ain't going nowhere."

"No, your house is down the street. This is my house!"

"My house!"

"Get out!"

"Move out the way so I can finish watching my show and stop with this foolishness. It's a real snore."

Raymond walked over to the television and turned it off.

"Have you lost your mind!" Victoria screamed.

"No, but you've obviously lost yours! Now, are you going to move, or do I have to do it?"

"Raymond, is this what you really want to do? Is it really what you want?"

"That's not the question. For months you've sat around and acted like Nigel, and I wasn't even here. You have already left us. I'm just trying to make it legal."

"That wasn't my question."

"Leave me alone…like you have for the last six months."

"Are you going to answer my question or not?"

"Get out isn't a good enough answer for you?"

"No, it's not. I want to hear you say it."

"You know I love you and never want you to leave, but I can't deal with this anymore. Every time something doesn't go your way, you get depressed. Where is your backbone? Where is your fight? I'm like a soldier on the battlefield alone because my battle buddy is dead and helpless," Raymond said as he went upstairs, not saying another word and leaving Victoria to that last thought.

She tried to act like this conversation didn't bother her, but it did, bothered her to the point where she could no longer enjoy the soap opera she was watching. Victoria tried to lay down on the couch, but she tossed and turned. It was all she could do because those last words Raymond spoke kept ringing through her ears.

The house is dark and silent; all you can hear is the wind whistling. Ray was upstairs and she thought Nigel was over a friend's. Victoria heard a noise coming from the kitchen but was scared to move. She laid still on the couch, waiting for the noise to stop, but whoever it was crept through the house and snuck up on her and patted her on the back, saying, "Victoria, wake up." She was startled, so much so that she almost peed on herself.

"Nigel, you scared the mess out of me! I didn't know you were here."

"I'm sorry, Victoria, but I need to talk to you."

"What is it, Nigel?"

"I know you miss ma, and so do I, but you have her house cleaner than you have your own. I don't know what went down between you two, but you can't let yourself go. And with all due respect, you have let yourself go, and it's embarrassing. My friends used to think you were hot, now they ask me what has happened to you. You need to get yourself together. I used to love it here but not so much anymore."

"I'm sorry to hear that but you don't understand."

"I understand more than you think. I may not know what it's like to be depressed, but I know what it's like to be angry. I know what it's like to want something so bad you can taste it, but it never makes it to your plate. I know what it's like to have to go on living despite the crap you have to deal with that life hands you, and you just want to die…I know."

"Yeah, I guess you do."

"I didn't say that to bring back up stuff, but I had to let you know where I was coming from."

"I know."

"Just think about it, okay. Dad loves you, and he doesn't want you to go anywhere."

"Oh, you heard that did you?"

"Yeah."

"Don't worry about it, Nigel. Your father and I are going to be okay. Now, go on back to bed and don't worry about us, okay."

"Alright, but seriously, do something with yourself."

Victoria thought long and hard about what she needed to do. Nigel was blunt, but she heard what he had to say. Raymond was too nice to say it that direct. She left and went to Niriya's house. Victoria realized what she had to do. In pajamas and all, she left the house and went upstairs to what used to be her parent's room. When she walked in, she became frightened, just like when she was a little girl being scolded by her mother's harsh words. Tears filled her eyes, and her lips started to tremble. Victoria fell to her knees as she had a flashback. "Momma, no! It wasn't me, momma! Momma!" "Shut up, lil girl. Let's see how you look bald-headed," her mother said as she dragged Victoria down the hallway to the bathroom and began cutting her long, beautiful hair. The haircut was horrendous, and she sent Victoria to school the next day and wouldn't fix her hair." Victoria cried the entire time, "Momma, stop! Please!"

"Victoria! Snap out of it!" Raymond said. Victoria was sobbing and shaking as she gripped to hug her husband and held onto him for dear life. She wouldn't let go.

"My God, what happened to you, Ria?" Raymond said asking but not asking and holding onto his wife.

"Take me home, please. Just take me home," Victoria said.

"Come on, honey," Raymond said as he picked his wife up off the floor.

Once they made it back to the house, Raymond said to Victoria, "Baby, this thing is bigger than you. It's something that you can't handle. It may be time for you to talk to someone."

"I wouldn't even know what to say or know where to begin," Victoria said.

"Just speak," Raymond said.

"I want this to be over with. I'm tired of holding onto this mess."

"Then take that first step."

"It seems like every time I want to move forward, there is a freight train pulling me back. When will it end?"

"The end begins with you, Ria."

"I don't know if I can do this, Ray."

"I'll be there with you every step of the way."

"So, you don't want me to leave?"

"Never did. I was hoping that would get you off your butt."

"Why would you do something so cold?"

"I tried everything else, and this was my last resort."

"I'm sorry I put you and Nigel through that. It was not my intention."

"Depression doesn't only hurt or affect you. It affects those around you, as well. Did you know that depression, weight gain, and stress are key factors in preventing pregnancies?"

"Where did you hear that?"

"I've studied it, and that is what I found out. We want to have a baby, and it will be done in God's timing; however, we can prepare and do things on our part to show God that we are ready for our blessing."

"I guess, but God doesn't need our help."

"True, but it's not about helping Him. It's about proving to him that we will take care of our blessing when He decides to bestow it on us. Faith without works is dead, and so is our faith without us working towards the promise."

"Hmmm…I can't even debate you on that."

"I'm glad you heard what I said."

"Not at first. Not last night."

"Then what led you to the house?"

"It was Nigel. He was blunt and harsh with words, but what I needed to hear."

"What did he say?"

"He said that I need to get myself together, and I let myself go," said Victoria.

"That would be him," Raymond said with a giggle.

"I know right."

As soon as morning hit, Victoria got herself together, cleaned the house, and found a psychiatrist. Her appointment is set for next week, but she scheduled a meeting with her pastor while she's waiting. He met with her right away. At the meeting, she shared some of what she's been going through in the meeting. Raymond was stunned at the things that were going on in her childhood. He didn't know how all that got past him when they grew up together. He knew her parents were strict, but since they we're wildin' out as teenagers, he didn't give it a second thought. The pastor asked a few questions and listened to what Victoria was saying. He concluded she is afraid of confrontation because of how her mother ruled the home. She was considered the "good girl" or "the perfect one," but realized she couldn't live up to her mother's expectations and was severely punished when she couldn't keep up with them.

Victoria scheduled many appointments with the psychiatrist for months and is still going. She gets the spiritual side from her pastor and the natural side of things from the psychiatrist and is getting along fine. Victoria found that she needed to talk about those things she had bottled up since she was a girl. Her mother was hellacious. She literally put the fear of God in her children. They were too scared to do anything; one was trying to get her love, and the other was trying to keep the "perfect" love going. This mother messed up her children.

Victoria is currently working hard. She's losing the weight she gained, focusing on Me, praying more, and finding herself in love with Me again. Her home was running smoothly, still no Niriya, and she was okay with that. Just like she needed help, she hoped her sister was getting that same aid. Raymond and Victoria are rekindling their love, and Nigel is still being Nigel.

In addition, Raymond has been working on his business after turning in his resignation. He is working from home. He has eight movie scripts that he's been writing over the years. They are ready to be put into action. He is working on buying a building right now, and Victoria is behind him one hundred percent.

Nigel is going to school but getting himself into a lot of trouble. His father realized he was having a hard time right now with his mother being gone and all. Raymond isn't really concerned, though; not in a bad way because he's there for Nigel and helps him get over this thing. They spend a lot of father-son time together, which helps him a lot.

The following Sunday, they all went to church, and the title of the lesson was "By This Time Next Year." Pastor Riley came from Genesis 18:10 NIV. "Everybody says, by this time next year," said Pastor Riley.

"By this time next year," repeated the congregation.

"This is the prophetic word of the Lord this morning. How many of you are still awaiting promises?" asked Pastor Riley. The congregation raised their hands and praised God.

"Yes, Lord," some of the congregation said.

"Bless your name, Jesus!" Sis Shanna said.

Victoria was quiet, almost like she lost faith in the promise. Raymond was just the same, not happy, or sad. They don't know what to believe anymore. Although they were disconnected, they still tuned into Pastor Riley's sermon.

"Turn to Genesis 18:10 in your Bibles," Pastor Riley said. As you could hear pages flipping throughout the sanctuary, Pastor Riley began to read the scripture. "And it reads, "And he said, I will certainly return unto thee according to the time of life; and, lo, Sarah thy wife shall have a son. And Sarah heard it in the tent door, which was behind him." God promised Abraham that he would have a son with his wife, Sarah. He sent his angel to let them know He was getting ready to make good on His promise. Some of you in here have been waiting for years and years for God to make His promise good. You have tarried, prayed, cried, and even given up on the promise. He doesn't hold it against you. It's giving Him a reason to show out in your life. When we read about Abraham and Sarah's life, you hardly find that they complained time and time again about the promised son. If we read further, we also find that Sarah laughed at what was said, then she lied about laughing when accused. Sarah had done some things in her life that wouldn't warrant a blessing. She gave her husband to their servant to have a son because she became impatient. After Hagar, the servant, became pregnant, she caused her to leave because Hagar was cruel to her. She regretted giving her husband to another woman, learning her lesson the hard way. Then if that wasn't enough, when the angel came down to tell them to get ready for the promise, she laughed. I mean busting a gut. She laughed so hard that the Angel of the Lord heard her from the tent. She had to be laughing hard, tears, and everything. I know it's funny, but it's real."

By this time, Victoria is squirming around in the pew, shrinking within the seat in shame. Nigel is looking at her, wondering if this was what happened with her and his mom. Raymond is still-faced and isn't giving away any of his thoughts. It's one uncomfortable situation, but everyone else was laughing at what the pastor was saying.

Pastor Riley continued to preach, "This is going to be short and sweet. God's prophecies never take long. All we have to do is accept the prophecy given. I know we had a good laugh at Sarah but doesn't that sound just like us when we become impatient. We make bad decisions and senseless choices that we regret then become discouraged with those decisions. Turn to Genesis 17:1-2. We often talk about Sarah's disbelief, but today, we're going to talk about Abram's. God is saying, Abram, can't handle what I'm about to do in his life. Abraham has to be the one to carry this out. Read verse five. The name must coincide with the promise. There is someone in here that has a decision to make about a change in their life. This is a man deciding. Let me tell you this, if God is giving you a decision to make, then there is obvious need for the change." "God, if this is you, make it plain for me," Raymond thought to himself.

Pastor Riley continued on with his sermon, "In verse fifteen, God had to even change Sarai's name for what she was about to birth. It takes two to manifest a thing. Abraham couldn't do it by himself, and neither could Sarah. They both needed each other. Abraham was the seed, Sarah was the fertile ground (womb), and God gave the increase. Sarah's womb was the incubator, and for something to incubate, a seed must be planted first. In verse one, God told Abram when he was ninety-nine years old that He is God and for him to walk before Him and be perfect. Now at this point, I can hear Abram taking his deep voice to a high pitch, saying, "God, what have I been doing the last decade? I mean, I'm saying, I'm ninety-nine years old…what else am I going to do?"

"I know that's right," one of the members said laughing.

The congregation was laughing hard and Pastor Riley had to bring back order, "Seriously though, Abraham was the first one to doubt and to laugh. It wasn't Sarah. He not only laughed, but he fell out laughing. Does the Bible not say he fell on his face and laughed?"

The congregation laughed some more.

"Come on now…it's like how y'all say…lmbo," Pastor Riley continued to say and chuckled a little bit himself. After everyone calmed down, Pastor Riley said, "Then he figured, forget the dumb stuff just do it through Ishmael, but God had to tell him, I will bless Ishmael, but my covenant is with Isaac. Men stop trying to pass the covenant off to someone who's not supposed to have it, nor are they conditioned or designed for it because of your unbelief. Trust God! I want all the men to come to the altar. Come on. This isn't a request…every man in this building, come to the altar. Get off the cameras and the doors, even my armor-bearers."

The men came up one by one. The altar was filled with men that had decisions to make. Pastor Riley began to pray over the men, "Lift your hands and surrender to God. It's between you and Him what you must decide on. Some of you have more than one decision to make. Father, help us to lean on you. As men, we are taught to do things independently and be the leader, but no one has hardly taught us to lean on You to help us be a man. Forgive us for doing these things on our own, doing our own will instead of Yours. We release to You right now every decision that we must make. We want You to invade our space. We want You to rule over us and be the head. We want the Holy Spirit to dwell within us. Father, fill and restore us again. We need you."

Some men were released, crying, and yielding, while others were being stubborn and stone-faced. Raymond was one of them. He knew I was talking to Him but still wasn't sure, and because I AM GOD, I made it plain to him.

Pastor Riley personally prayed over the men that I instructed him to. He made it to Raymond, who was daring him to act like he would speak for God. Pastor Riley said, "Before I began to give you what God has given me for you, you need to know that, yes, I am God's microphone. He does and will speak through me to give a word to you. When I speak this word, it's up to you to decide what you will do with it. Do you understand?"

"Yes," Raymond said.

"You were the man God was talking about earlier. You have a decision to make; actually, a few. You have made decisions before without God and look at the place it has you. He wants you to make these next decisions with Him. Whether it's right or wrong, the decisions you make will affect the rest of your life and your family's," Pastor Riley said.

Raymond's eyes began to well up with tears. He lifted his hands and closed his eyes.

Pastor Riley had someone to take away the microphone. He doesn't like giving anyone prophecies over the mic because he believes it's a personal encounter. He spoke to Raymond, "Now, you are ready to receive what God has for you. Do not fear what God wants to do in your wife. There is a reason He has waited to bless you all with a baby, and it will be revealed in time, but now is the time for preparation. By this time next year, you and Victoria will have a son. God says to you, Raymond, "As I told Abraham, now I'm telling you, I will bless her and give you a son also of her. Victoria will bear you a son for sure, and you shall call him Michael." Do not tell Victoria. God will reveal it to her in His timing. You prepare. You build the nursery. You buy the clothes. You do it and watch what God does," Pastor Riley prophesied.

At this point, Raymond was like jello. His legs wobbled him right to the floor. He released himself to Me and rededicated his life to Me. After he got up off the floor, Pastor Riley looked at him, winked, and smiled as Raymond returned to his seat. My presence was so upon him that he could not speak to his wife until a few hours after they got home. Victoria understood he was in My presence, so she didn't bother him. She warmed up the dinner she had prepared the night before. Nigel didn't know what was going on, and on top of that, he was missing his mom. Raymond took the guest bedroom and started moving things out of it. Victoria couldn't fathom what he was doing, but she left him alone. Today is the day that began the change of his family's life.

Love No Longer Waits

"Raymond, I've held my tongue long enough. What do you think you are doing?" Victoria asked as she walked past the old guest room.

"What are you talking about, Ria?" Raymond rebutted.

"For the last three months, you have made a nursery out of this room. Are you taunting me? This is cruel…even for you," Victoria said as she turned away from him to walk out of the room.

"Baby, please believe me when I say it's nothing like that at all. If we are going to believe for a baby, we must be prepared for it," Raymond said.

"It's been so long, plus I am forty-six years old, and I've come to the decision that I don't even want a baby anymore. I'd rather start working on my career. Something ought to bring me some joy," Victoria foolishly stated.

Raymond grabbed his wife and said, "Victoria, you don't mean that. Don't give up on God. Even during the irrational statement you just made, He still hasn't given up on you. I promise you this is not a taunt. Baby, just trust me on this…okay," Raymond pleaded and was doing the best he could to not to tell his wife what God said.

Victoria's eyes filled with tears in hopes that her husband was right. She said, "Fine, but I'm not going to stand idly by and wait around for this to happen."

"That's all I'm asking, sweetheart," Raymond said.

He came out the room and closed the door behind him while Victoria went into their bedroom and shut the door behind her. Nigel was in school, so Raymond figured this would be a good time to woo his wife or at least try because she's in one of her funky moods. He opened the door and said, "Ria, get dressed. I'm going to take you out for lunch."

"Where are we going?"

"Just get dressed. Put on something casual."

"Alright."

"Don't take forever either."

"Alright!"

Raymond closed the door behind him, laughing at his wife. She trips him out with her attitudes. He often wondered had she gone through menopause and didn't tell him.

Thirty minutes passed before Victoria came downstairs. Raymond said to her, "It's about time."

"Perfection takes time," she answered.

"And you are perfect," he said.

"You so full of it."

"Well, then let me empty myself."

"Eww…nasty."

"Naw, just being real."

"In due time, sir; in due time."

They both laughed and left the house. They had a few hours left before Nigel came home from school. Raymond took his wife to a spa. She was in heaven. They both got a massage. She wanted them both to get a pedicure, but Raymond declared that no one was going to touch his feet. As a result, she was the only one to get a pedicure. They went to the bar and drank a couple of virgin daiquiris, had a lovely cuisine, and went and played an interesting game of golf. They made a small wager. While they were out, Nigel called, asking if he could stay after school for the basketball game. This excited Raymond because now his wife can make good on her bet.

Considering the small window of opportunity, Raymond rushed his wife home. She didn't know what was going on. Victoria was a little upset about losing the game. She is a bit of a competitor and sore loser. Raymond didn't care. He always laughed at his wife's antics. All he knew was that she better make good on her bet, and it best be as soon as they get home. As soon as they walked through the doors, Raymond clapped his hands together and said, "Let's run it!"

Victoria couldn't do anything but laugh because she knew what time it was. She said, "I don't know why you are in a rush because it's not like you can handle it anyway."

"Oh, is that a challenge?" he asked.

"You tell me," she responded.

"Ria, don't play. You already know the game."

"Uhm…must not have been a good game because I can't remember anything."

"Oh, yeah," Raymond said as he chased his woman through the house. Victoria was laughing and could hardly get away from him. After a few minutes of chasing, Raymond sat on the couch and said, "Man, I'm too old for these cat and mouse games."

Victoria laughed and said, "I told you."

"Oh, don't trip. You are going to give it up."

"Ray, if you tired now, what makes you think that you can even roll your "vehicle" into my garage."

"You got jokes. Never mind all that. Your time is up, and so is this game. Let's get it poppin' lil ma."

"Alright, give me a minute," Victoria said as she went upstairs.

He rested on the couch while waiting on Victoria. She really didn't want to do it because it made her feel uncomfortable. She had never done anything like this before, nor did she think this was something that a Christian woman should be doing. There were mixed emotions about it, but I gave her comfort. I told her it was okay, and if that's what he wanted, give in to him.

Following My comfort, she went downstairs after putting the music in the sound system. It was a slow song. When Raymond saw her, he almost gave in and didn't want her to complete the bet. He was stunned to see his wife walking down the steps in black stilettos with rhinestones on them, flawless hair (she put on her long straight wig for this one), a sexy, sensual pink and black negligee, and jewelry to compliment her night attire. She told him to come and sit in the oversized sofa chair. She glided to the music dancing in front of him and the soft sensual scent of cucumber body spray would sashay across his nostrils. He was so turned on he didn't know what to do. Victoria found herself immensely enjoying this bet and turning on her husband. The slow song went off, and another song came on (to surprise him)…I'm A Savage. She moved her body in ways to the beat and to the words that he'd never seen before; then, it was all he wrote. That was it! He was out of the game!!! He didn't even let her finish the song out.

After he snatched her up in his arms and carried her upstairs, they made their own music in their bedroom. Love was in the air. They let go of the past and thought only of each other. Raymond enjoyed his wife. He loves her smile and laughter. He wasn't used to the woman who became bitter and depressed and conniving, then one day up and one day down. It was a lot for him to deal with, and he didn't know how. All he knew was that he had to build her up.

Once they were finished, it was about time to pick up Nigel from school. At first, Victoria wasn't going to go, but Raymond wanted her to. When they got to the school, Nigel was nowhere to be found. There was no one on school grounds. Raymond called Nigel's cell phone, but no answer. Victoria was about to become unglued because here they go again; just when she and Raymond got on track, something crazy popped off. She was tired of things being this way, but she remembered what Raymond said about being up and down. This time she prayed within herself, asking Me to help them with this situation. They called all his friends, but they said they didn't know where he was. Raymond was ready to snap. Come to find out, after talking to his friends, Nigel never made it to school that day. They went home after finding out this information. It was six o'clock in the evening, and the only time they heard from him was when he called asking to stay after school. They knew he was having problems, but this was ridiculous. He's been through worse things. They waited to call the police to file a missing person report, holding off for at least another hour.

After about forty-five minutes after coming home, they received a phone call from Nigel, "Pops, I'm ready for you to pick me up."

"Where are you at?" Raymond asked.

"I'm at school, Pop," Nigel said.

"Oh, okay. The game is over already?" Raymond asked playing dumb.

"Yeah, and it was a good game too, but we lost," Nigel said not having a clue.

"I'm on my way," said Raymond.

"Okay but hurry up because I'm almost the last person here," Nigel said.

Raymond hung up the phone, looked at his wife, and said, "Ria, this boy must think I'm stupid."

"What did he say?" she asked.

"He said it was a good game, and they just let out. Then on top of that, he told me to hurry up because he's about to be the last one there," he said.

"No, he didn't."

"Yes, he did. I'm going to kill 'em."

"Calm down, baby. He's going through a lot. Let him have this one."

"Ain't no way Ria…ain't no way."

"What I'm saying is, talk to him about what he just pulled but don't go hard on him."

"I've been nothing but nice for these past couple of years, and I've had it. This is the last straw."

"Come on, let's just go get him."

"You stay here because I need to handle this."

"I want to go."

"I'm not going to hurt him, Ria."

"I think you will because you are upset."

"I got it. Let me handle it."

"Okay, but call me to let me know that everything is okay."

"I will," Raymond said as he kissed his wife goodbye.

Victoria was on pins and needles waiting on the phone call. She just knew Raymond was going to kill that boy. He was fuming. He could not believe what was going on. On top of that, blowing the good day he was having with his wife. I used this time to talk with Victoria. She is so frantic about what would happen that she didn't know what to do with herself. "Victoria, go into the room that your husband has been fixing up," I spoke to her heart.

"Lord, I can't. I just can't," she said.

"Just go," I said to her.

"God, I don't know why you are doing this to me. You know I can't handle this right now."

"Would you trust Me?"

"I can't."

"Am I not God? Do I not know what I'm doing? Did I not create the earth and everything in it?"

"Yes, Lord. You know, I know that."

"Then trust Me."

Reluctantly Victoria went into the room, and when she opened the door, she was wowed. It was as if her eyes were opened to a brand-new world. She noticed the hard work her husband put into the room. He had diapers in the closet ranging from newborn to six months, and there were many of them. He painted the room a baby blue color and placed designs on the wall. He even put a rocking chair in the corner of the room with a small rectangle coffee table next to it. "Raymond put a lot of thought into this room, didn't he, Lord?" Victoria said to Me.

"Yes, he did," I answered.

"Wow! I'm like blown away. I've never looked at the work he did," she said.

"Why do you think he did this?" I asked her.

"I don't know. That's what puzzles me. It doesn't make sense."

"You don't have a clue, do you?"

"Lord, you know I don't."

"You were blinded by the pain of not having a baby that you didn't want to see what was unraveling right in front of your eyes."

"Could you blame me?"

"I can understand, but if you had trusted Me, you wouldn't have had to endure unnecessary pain."

"You could have told me that I was going to be old and decrepit before I had a child. That would have been nice to know."

"You are not too old for Me to use you, and you are not decrepit! Let Me use you. There is a reason for what you call a delay, but it's not a delay. It's all about My timing."

"So, Lord, what are you saying?"

"You will see soon enough."

"Is that an answer? Is that all?"

"Isn't it enough?"

"I don't feel like that's an answer, Lord."

"It's good enough."

"If you say so."

Victoria continued to go through the room and marvel at the work her husband had done. She started moving some things around, took blankets out of the plastic, and placed them in the wall unit with built-in dressers and closets. She hung up some of the clothes and then rested in the rocking chair. This day, Victoria was at peace with waiting patiently for their baby boy. She rocked back and forth in the chair with her eyes closed, visualizing holding her son.

An hour had passed before the telephone rang. It was Raymond, and he was steaming. Victoria was still at peace handling the matter. Nigel was in the background going off, and Raymond was about to "get with him." Victoria jumped in her car to meet up with them, but she stopped and changed her mind. Instead, she asked Raymond to put Nigel on the phone.

"Yeah," Nigel disrespectfully said.

"Yeah! I told you not to disrespect my wife," Raymond yelled in the background.

"Man, I ain't trying to hear all that," Nigel said.

"Nigel, talk to me. What is going on with you?" Victoria asked.

"Ya man is going off ova hear, and I ain't tryin' to hear that noise he talkin'," Nigel said.

"Look, Nigel, I want you to be truthful with me, okay," she said.

"A'ight," he replied.

"Did you get busted?" she asked.

"Yeah," he answered.

"Then why are you arguing with your dad if you know you did wrong? How do you expect for him to react," she asked?

"He didn't give me a chance to tell my side of the story. He believed what somebody else said and that's not right," Nigel said.

"Did you ditch school today?" Victoria asked.

"No, I didn't. I was at school today, all day. Call tomorrow and check for yourself. I don't know who told y'all that, but when I find out, I'm going to put 'em in a ditch," Nigel said.

"Don't say that because you're not going to do that," she said.

"You can believe that if you want," Nigel said.

"Was there a football game?" she asked.

"No. I did lie about that, but I was at school today," he said.

"Where were you then? We came up to the school looking for you, and when we didn't see anyone, we became worried. You had us in agony. We were about to call the police if you hadn't called within the hour. We love you, Nigel, and we don't want anything to happen to you," she said.

"I know, and I'm sorry," Nigel said.

"Look, this is what I want you to do. Apologize to your father when we get off the phone. Do not be disrespectful and keep a tight lid on that mouth of yours, and I will talk to your dad when y'all get home, okay," Victoria said.

"Yes, ma'am," Nigel said.

"Alright, I will see you when you get here. I love you," she said.

"I love you too, Victoria," he replied.

They hung up the phone, and she eagerly awaited their arrival, deciding not to go and meet them after all. Victoria knew it wouldn't be anything nice when they got home, so she began to pray over her house, over Nigel's room, and their bedroom. She was determined that this night would end with just as much peace as it started.

Once they got home, Victoria heard a door slam. Nigel went straight to his room and closed the door, and Raymond came upstairs to find his wife in the room he'd been preparing for the last three months. It brought a big smile to his face. It was so peaceful in the room. She was still in the rocking chair swaying away.

"Man, this was the last thing I expected to find when I got home," Raymond said.

"I love what you've done in here," Victoria said.

"Baby, you look so peaceful rocking in that chair. This room fits you," he said.

"I want to thank you, Ray."

"Thank me for what?"

"Preparing this room, no matter the many roadblocks I tried to put up. I never really looked at the room until tonight, and it was here that I found peace. It was here I was affirmed about our son. I don't know when, but I know that God will do it. I never would have come in here and found the peace I now have had you not made this room."

"I only do what I'm told."

"Good thing too, because who would have known that the very thing I detested would be the very thing that would bring me peace."

"I'm glad to see you in here and even put some of the things up and added a little of your own flavor to it. That's what I had been praying for...."

"What's that?"

"Every time I came in here to work, I would pray over the baby's things, the room, me and you, and that you would take the time to come in here and take part in building up the nursery."

Raymond was happy. It took his mind off Nigel's foolishness. It caused him to regain focus and calm down a little. He was still "38 hot" about what Nigel did, but his wife and unborn son were all he could think about right now.

Later that night, Victoria went into Nigel's room, checked on him, kissed him goodnight, and told him she loved him. Then she went into her room and got in the bed with Raymond. "Raymond, let's go to sleep and deal with this tomorrow," Victoria said. "Alright," Raymond said. She caressed her husband until he fell asleep. She quietly prayed over his mind and heart, then fell asleep herself.

The next morning, Raymond got up and fixed Victoria breakfast in bed. She woke up to her favorite cereal, a carnation on the corner of the tray, a parfait, and a glass of orange juice. "Ria, wake up," Raymond said, wearing his silk robe with it halfway opened.

"Awh, aren't you sweet. Thank you, baby," Victoria said.

"You're welcome," Raymond said.

"Are you going to eat with me?"

"No, not this time. I'm going to get Nigel up and take him to school."

"Raaaay…"

"I'm good, Ria. I'm good."

"You sure?"

"Yes, I'm sure."

"Okay, now because I don't want to have to come and get you out of jail."

"You are not going to have to do that. I'm going to talk to him, father to son, and he's going to have to understand that he can't just do what he wants to do and not receive the repercussions behind it."

"Ray, he didn't have a problem with that. He didn't feel like you gave him a chance. He said he was at school all day yesterday."

"Well, I'm going to check to make sure."

"I was going to call this morning myself."

"You won't have to because I'm all over it. Let me handle him, and you eat your breakfast."

"Alright, but take it easy on him."

"Not making any promises."

Raymond woke Nigel up and took him to school. He ate breakfast with him and had a long and serious father-son talk with Nigel. He was a little bit more receptive about the conversation this morning. Raymond's intrigue was the whereabouts of Nigel yesterday.

"You will be mad if I tell you," Nigel said.

"I'm already mad as it is, so you might as well tell me," Raymond said.

"Pops, you remember the first day I came back here, and we went to the burger joint?" Nigel asked.

"Yes. What about it?" Raymond said.

"Do you remember the chick at the counter, Sasha?"

"Yes, Sasha, she's a sweet girl; always nice."

"We have been going out for a year, and I was over her house. We stayed after school together."

"Nigel, what did you do? Better yet, did you use protection?"

"No, sir," Nigel said as he put his head down.

"Dawggone Nigel, I told you that you are too young to be having sex."

"She's the only one I've been with since I've been here."

"Doesn't matter. Are you ready to be a father if she becomes pregnant? Are you ready for sexually transmitted diseases just in case you are not the only one she's slept with or anyone else you've slept with? Are you ready for the emotional attachments?"

"That's my girl, Pops. I pull out and the only one she's with."

"Time will tell. Let me get you to school."

"Aye pops, don't be mad."

"It's hard not to be. We are going to have to meet her parents and monitor you guys better."

"You want to meet her parents?"

"Yes, and you will have to tell her parents that you are having sex with their daughter."

"What?"

"Yes, sir, you said you are ready for the emotional attachment, and with that comes responsibility. Being accountable allows her parents to choose to put her on birth control or not, and if they want her alone with you or other measures. Neither one of y'all are old enough to take care of any babies. Having a baby comes with financial responsibilities, maturity, generational bloodlines…."

"Generational bloodlines? What's that?"

"The blood and genes that flow from both the father and mother into the baby. Generational bloodlines and connections are especially important. You gotta know who and what you are connecting to because it will affect how you raise your child, what the child will endure and or carry, and what you will have to fight as a parent. Y'all youngsters think you're ready for adult responsibilities when you have trouble managing your own teenage responsibilities. Creating a baby is easy, but maintaining a family is hard, and you of all people should know that."

"Man, bump all that, dad, and I sho' can't tell her parents we had sex."

"Well then, if you can't do that, what makes you think you can handle the liabilities of having sex with this girl?"

"Can you just take me to school already?"

"I most certainly can."

"Dad, you be trippin'."

"How long have you two been having sex?"

"I don't know. It's been a while."

"I ought to wring your neck."

"It's all good. She good peoples, Pops. All them girls at my school know you got money and that's all they want. They stuck up gold diggas, and I 'on trust 'em."

"I know Sasha is a sweet girl, and if I had to choose someone for you, she'd be it. The problem I have is that you kept this a secret, and y'all are too young to be doing all this."

"It wasn't a secret; I just didn't tell you. Ma knew."

"Why wouldn't you tell me?"

"I 'on know, just didn't come up."

"Hmm…"

"Look, Pops, me and Sasha straight. Ain't nothing gone happen."

Raymond eventually dropped Nigel off at school and found out he was telling the truth about being there yesterday. However, Raymond couldn't believe what he had just heard and how naïve Nigel was about sex. He had plans to set things in motion to teach him a lesson. Nigel isn't going to know what hit him.

Victoria was at home working on her interior decorating designs. She is quite creative and makes exquisite designs from nothing.

Raymond called Victoria on his way home to set up Nigel and told her what had happened. "Ria, you are not going to believe this."

"What?"

"On the way to the school, I asked Nigel where he was yesterday, and he said with Sasha."

"From the burger place?"

"Yes, and apparently, they are having sex and have been for almost a year."

"For real? Lawd Jesus."

"Then he told me I'm making too big a deal out of it. Can you believe that?"

"How does he expect you to react?"

"I don't know, but I have a plan to help him out."

"What do you mean by that?"

"We are going to present a situation to him."

"I don't know if I like the sound of this."

"Ria, the boy has got to learn. He thinks he can just do what he wants and not be punished for it. I don't know what Niriya taught him, but it's got to be drilled out of him."

"That's good and all but I'm concerned about this plan you are cooking up."

"It's nothing to worry about, Ria. All I want to know is, are you going to back me up?"

"You know I will but it can't be anything too crazy."

They said their goodbyes and got off the phone. Raymond put his plan in motion, hoping it would be an eye-opener for Nigel. Little did Raymond know; Nigel's mind was on telling Sasha's parents all through the school day. Raymond wouldn't care. He would still do this plan to drive it home.

Victoria called Leigha and told her what was going on. Leigha couldn't believe it and was so in shock, and the plan was so gangsta that she couldn't turn down the opportunity to be part of this plan. She was all in, and her husband Joshua too. The plan was in motion. When Nigel hits the house, he has a huge surprise waiting on him. Leigha also told Victoria that she has something she wants to tell Victoria.

Meanwhile, Victoria took a break from the scheme and looked over boy names for her son. She enjoyed herself, finding out the meanings of the names and looking through all of them. She had a few in mind that she wrote down and present it to Raymond. She saw some little girls' names too that she loved. Victoria didn't mind having a little "her" around. She figured, if it took this long just to get a son, there was no telling if it would take forever for her to get pregnant again or if she would even have another baby ever. Nevertheless, she still committed some names to memory.

After that, Victoria started working on some decorations for their son's room. This was so exciting for her. Then she went to the gym to do her daily exercise. She loved her instructor. Maria was so motivating. Victoria was losing weight, loving how she felt on the inside, and learning some sexy Latin dance moves. Her confidence was building more and more as she kept attending her classes.

As time got closer for Nigel to come home, Victoria started winding down to put everything into play. She went ahead and prepared dinner like she usually does. She hadn't seen Raymond all day. It was a good thing they had breakfast together, or else she wouldn't have seen him then either. Raymond was looking forward to putting his plan into action. Nigel was on pins and needles because he didn't know how to tell Sasha's parents that he was sexin' their daughter.

Around 4:00 PM, Nigel and Raymond walked through the door and you could feel the tension. Everyone spoke with "niceities" and went on about their evening. Nigel could feel something was going on, but he just couldn't put his finger on it. He was smiling and playing nice to ease whatever blow was coming. No one mentioned his talk with his father earlier that morning, which seemed a little odd. Later that evening, Victoria called everyone for dinner. The dinner table was quiet. Then Raymond busts out with a question that just about knocked Nigel out of his seat, "Did you know that Sasha is pregnant?"

Nigel, stunned at first, says, "Stop tha cap. She would've told me. I knew something was strange. You playin' a trick on me."

"I'm serious. This is not a game," Raymond said.

"Yeah, right. Look Pops, I know I have to tell Sasha's parents, and this is just a scare tactic," Nigel said shrugging off what his father was doing, but Raymond wasn't worried at all.

"Let's call her then," Raymond said as he pulled out his phone.

"How did you get her number," Nigel asked.

"Her father called me earlier today. This is what happens when you play a grown folk's game," Raymond said.

"Uh, huh," Victoria said.

Raymond dialed the number and put the phone up to his ear. Nigel is starting to think that just maybe this is real. Raymond said, "Hello, Mr. Inez. This is Raymond Johnson, Nigel's father."

"Pop, this isn't funny anymore. Hang up the phone," Nigel said.

"Sit down and be quiet," Victoria said. This was new to him because Victoria had never been stern with him, and that is when he realized that this wasn't a joke.

"My son didn't believe me and my wife when we told him that Sasha is pregnant. Can you please put her on the phone so she can tell him?" Raymond asked.

Raymond handed Nigel the phone, and he said, "Sasha?"

"Hey Nigel," she said.

"What's wrong with your voice?" Nigel asked due to her Latin accent coming through heavily.

"I've been crying all day. I got sick at school and thought it was the flu. My dad picked me up from school and took me to the doctor, and that was when I found out I didn't have the flu but that I was pregnant," Sasha said.

"Sasha, if this is a joke, it's not funny," Nigel said.

"It's not a joke Nigel. This is serious. What are we going to do?" Sasha asked.

"I don't know," Nigel said with his stomach in knots.

"My dad wants to speak with you," Sasha said.

"Why? What does he want to speak to me for?" he asked.

"Why do you think?" she replied.

"Alright, put him on," he said.

"Nigel," Mr. Inez said.

"Yes, sir," Nigel said.

"I let you into my house and date my daughter and this is how you do me? You knock her up?" Mr. Inez asked.

"No, sir. I didn't…I don't…I didn't mean. I'm sorry," Nigel said.

"So, what are you going to do about this?" asked Mr. Inez.

"I don't know, sir, but I will figure out something," Nigel said.

"You right. You are going to figure something out because she will not raise this baby on her own," said Joshua, who's pretending her father.

"I know, sir. I'm sorry," Nigel said.

"It's too late for sorry. I want to hear a plan," her father said.

"I don't have a plan. I just found out a few minutes ago. I mean, what do you want me to do. I can't whip out a plan at the drop of a dime," Nigel said.

"You trying to buck up at me? I ought to come over there and break your neck," Mr. Inez said.

"For what?" Nigel asked.

"For what? Well, for starters, getting my daughter pregnant, betraying my trust, having sex with my Sasha behind my back, disrespecting my house and my rules, and that's just to name a few," Mr. Inez said.

"Can I call you tomorrow once I come up with a plan? At least give me that," said Nigel.

"Well, that's all you got. I will see you tomorrow at my house after school," Mr. Inez said.

"Ok. Can I speak to Sasha, please?" Nigel asked.

"No, you may not. You may talk to her after you talk to me about your plan," Mr. Inez said.

"I understand. Can you at least tell her that I love her, and I will talk to her tomorrow?" Nigel asked.

"I don't owe you anything. I will tell her if I decide to," said Mr. Inez.

"That's fine. Goodbye, Mr. Inez," Nigel said but Mr. Inez just hung up the phone.

Nigel was so scared when he got off that phone that he ran to use the bathroom before he used it on himself. He ran, saying not a word to his dad or Victoria. Raymond loved every bit of this lesson he was teaching. Victoria was hoping they didn't go overboard but does see how it can help. Nigel was vomiting and had the runs (the bubble guts). He was scared. He never felt like this before, and he wishes he could turn back time because he would have listened to his father.

"Nigel, are you coming back down to eat?" Victoria asked, but he didn't respond.

"You need to come back because we are not finished talking to you," Raymond said, and still no response.

Nigel came out a few minutes later and said, "Can I be excused from the table? I've got a lot to think about and little time to do it in."

"No, because you have to answer our questions first," Raymond said.

"Honey, are you alright?" Victoria asked Nigel being concerned this was now going too far.

"Yes, ma'am. I'm fine," Nigel said.

"Yeah…you humble now," his father said.

"Ray! That's enough," Victoria said hitting his leg.

"He's alright, Ria!" her husband replied.

"Pop, what more do we need to talk about right now? I've just got some wild news, and my mind is somewhere else," Nigel said.

"Look, son, I'm going to give you some space, but I want your cell phone. You will not be making any calls tonight. The phone is mine and no internet privileges either," Raymond said handing out punishment.

"I don't even want to talk to nobody right now," Nigel said.

"Go on upstairs Nigel. We will check on you in a little bit," Victoria said.

He left the table and the food on his plate. He lost his appetite…kind of feeling like Samson; all his strength was gone. All sorts of questions ran through his head, and he couldn't develop any type of plan. Nigel tried to sleep but couldn't do that either. He tossed and turned the whole night. He wished he could talk to Sasha, but he had already crossed her father's boundaries, and he didn't want to add to the fire. This is the last thing he wanted —to be a father at seventeen years old. He'd be eighteen by the time the baby was born, but that was still young. More so than that, he knew once his mom returned, if she returned, she would kill him. Nigel had no clue what to do.

Raymond and Victoria cleaned the kitchen and went to bed talking about the nights' festivities.

"Ray, I didn't know we were going to let him go to sleep on this."

"Baby, I want it to stew overnight. I want him to toss and turn thinking about how his life is going to change with a baby on the way."

"Yeah, but did you see his face? He was pale and sickly."

"You know what? Earlier, he said he could handle it. Now I'm giving it to him raw and uncut. He needs to recognize he is not grown."

"I understand that, but I believe he's learned his lesson."

"Ria, let me do my job as a father. I have to break this down to him father to son style, or he won't get it."

"I guess you are right. I hope you are right."

"Oh, you better trust that he is in there thinking about some things."

"I bet he is."

"Joshua and Leigha were great, weren't they?"

"Yes, they were good…a little too good."

"I may have to pay them for outstanding service."

"You are so crazy."

"And I'm about to get crazier, Cupcake."

"Oh, gawd. Why you say that?"

"Because we finna make a baby of our own."

"That's sick. How are you even in the mood?"

"Why not? I'm legal both spiritually and naturally, on paper and in heaven. I'm good."

"You see, you are triflin' for saying something like that."

"Then, why are you laughing?"

"Do you even have to ask? You are crazy, and something is really wrong with you."

Raymond was serious about making love and gave Victoria foreplay until she gave in, which didn't take much. Nigel was grossed out all over again because he could hear them. With the present predicament, the last thing he wanted to hear was sex…especially sex from "old" people.

The next day was on the horizon, and Nigel was dreading it. He didn't like waking up from a horrible night's sleep only to face a day of the unknown. His head was so screwed up that he wished he were a virgin again. Then only moments after waking up, there was a knock on his door. His father woke him up to take him to school and reveal the scheme they played on him. Raymond was hard but not that hard to where his son's mind couldn't be on his schoolwork. All Raymond wanted to do was make Nigel realize there are consequences from his choices.

On the drive to school, Nigel quickly said, "Pop, I'm so sorry for not listening to you. I wish I could go back. This is not what I want."

"I know it's not, son, but you have to know that with every wrong choice you make…," Raymond said as he was cut off by Nigel.

"There are consequences. I know, Pop," Nigel said.

"You seem sincere," Raymond said.

"I am," Nigel said.

"Well, I'm going to turn back the hands of time for you," his father said.

"What do you mean?" Nigel asked.

"Sasha isn't pregnant. That wasn't even Sasha on the phone."

"Who was it?"

"It was Joshua and Leigha."

"Awh, that was dirty and low down, but I understand why you did it."

"Do you?"

"Yeah, I mean…man…I'm too happy to be mad at the fact y'all played me. I got to tell Jesus thank ya!"

"That ain't funny."

"Then why you laughin' Pop?"

"Alright, alright, alright, it was funny, but son, even though Sasha isn't pregnant, we still have to meet her parents, and you are still going to have to let them know you all had sex."

"Seriously?"

"Dead serious."

"Well, I guess I'd rather tell that news than the other, but we ain't goin' to have to worry about sex…at least on my part…for a long time. I don't have nothing left in me."

"I'm glad we have an understanding, son. Have a good day at school."

"A'ight, pop," Nigel said as he got out of the car.

Raymond called Victoria as soon as he dropped Nigel off at school and told her all that happened. She was relieved her husband let him off the hook.

The following week, Raymond and Victoria met Sasha's parents. They weren't happy at all hearing their daughter was having sex. However, they are glad that responsible parents brought it to their attention. Sasha and Nigel are still dating but with chaperones. Nigel wasn't a tad bit turned on. He kept envisioning being a father at seventeen. He was literally scared straight.

Nigel finished the next three months of the school year trouble-free and was thankful for summer vacation. Then, about a week ago, Leigha told Victoria that she was seven weeks pregnant. Although Victoria is genuinely happy for her best friend, part of her was sadden. Niriya still hasn't returned. Raymond purchased a building and built a few studios within the building. Victoria still works from home but is lucrative in her business. She decorated the nursery, redid her bedroom and guest bathroom, took pictures, provided some pro bono work, and showed them to potential clients. They admired her work and hired her instantly. She is in love with what she is doing. While she works from home, she put Nigel in a music camp during the summer. He's excited about it. She was elevated to an auxiliary leader at church of the decorating committee, and she hasn't been happier. Victoria lost a lot of weight by the time late June hit. She felt great because she was looking fabulous and feeling sexy. She bought herself a new wardrobe and constantly continues to work out. However, two months ago, Victoria had to start taking it easy because she found out she was pregnant! Leigha is only a few weeks more pregnant than her bestie. They are pregnant at the same time and they are milking it for all it's worth.

They made all kinds of plans because now they can plan birthdays together, schedule playdates, and get them into the same daycare and schools. The timing was perfect!

Enjoying the Love

Nine and a half months later, the ladies are ready to meet their babies. Joshua and Leigha had their daughter a few weeks ago. They named her Ja'Miya Faith. Does it need to be said that Raymond and Victoria are the Godparents? Now, it's Victoria and Raymond's turn. They enjoyed the nine-month pregnancy every step of the way, even the morning sickness, and in just a few hours, Victoria will give birth to their son. Raymond is by her side, being her rock when she needs it and her cheerleader when she wants to quit because the pain is excruciating. It's just about time for Victoria to start pushing.

"Come on, baby, you can do this," Raymond said.
"Alright, Victoria, let's push," said the doctor.
"One, two, three!" said the nurse and doctor.
After pushing for a while, the doctor said, "We're almost there. Just one more push."
"I can't. I'm so tired," Victoria said.
"Ria, you can do it. Come on, baby," Raymond said.
"Okay," she responded.
"One, two, three," then out popped their newborn son, letting out a cry.
"Congratulations on your new baby boy," the doctor said. The nurses cleaned him off and presented him to his parents.

They held their son and Victoria cried. She couldn't believe she was holding her son in her arms. Her family is now complete. Nothing else mattered. It was as if she was in the room alone. There was no noise, no one in the room. It was just her and her son. If she could have gotten out of her bed and danced around the room with him in her arms, she would have but pain out of nowhere consumed the solidarity state she was in with her son. She let out a loud scream. "What's the matter, Ria?" Raymond asked.

"I don't know. I just feel the need to push again," she answered.
"Nurses, we're going to have to go into surgery stat," the doctor said.
"What's going on, doc?" Raymond asked concerned.
"She has another baby in there, but it's in distress. She's starting to bleed a lot," the doctor answered.
"Is my wife going to be okay?" Raymond asked.
"I'm going to do all I can," the doctor answered.

They headed into surgery quickly. Victoria wondered why everything for her had to come with more pain than anyone else. She couldn't understand why she just couldn't push out the other baby like everyone else. She has to have problems with the birth. Tears began to slowly slide down each side of her face. The nurse that was holding her hand saw it and wiped it away. She said to Victoria, "Now is not the time to cry. Now is the time for you to pray the prayers I know you've been known to pray. God is going to bring you and the baby out safe, sound, and blessed." Victoria closed her eyes and began to pray to her Father. Afterward, her tears dried up, and she was in a deep, sedated sleep.

Moments later, the baby was cut out of Victoria. However, they had to take the baby and keep going because she was still bleeding internally. They put her under, but this is where it gets interesting. Her heartbeat was fluctuating rapidly, her vitals unstable. The doctors and nurses steadily tried to get her stabilized. After working on her for hours, Victoria's vitals and heartbeat were fine and stabilized. They stopped the bleeding, stitched her up, and placed her in ICU due to the extent of the surgery, and weren't sure if she'd wake up right away. Plus, they wanted to keep a close eye on her.

Raymond sat by Victoria's bedside and held her hand. They wouldn't allow the babies in ICU; therefore, Raymond had to go to the nursery, spend time with the babies, and feed them. She moaned a lot in her sleep. He didn't understand it but watched her closely. She was out for the rest of the day. He went to check on the babies. Nigel stayed in the room with her while his dad was gone. He didn't let on, but he was worried about her. Nigel was scared. He's now a big brother and thought about being an example for them, but he also wondered if he would now be put on the back burner because of them. Nigel was conflicted in his soul. He wanted to do good but wasn't sure what that would bring.

The next morning, Nigel was back in the room with Victoria while his father checked on the babies. He noticed her starting to move around. She was making small noises and turning her head. He got up and walked to stand beside her. She mumbled words he couldn't understand. Then she opened her eyes.

"Mom," Nigel said softly.

"Nigel," Victoria struggled to say, not realizing she had a tube in her throat and was unable to utter a word.

"Are you okay?" Nigel asked. She shook her head yes. He called his dad to let him know Victoria was awake. He let her know that Raymond was checking on the babies. Victoria had a puzzled look on her face when Nigel said, babies. Raymond rushed upstairs, and the nurse came in to check on her.

"How are you feeling, Victoria?" the nurse asked. All she could do was give a thumbs up. "We didn't expect you to wake up this quickly. It's good to see you doing well. What is your pain level? Show me with your fingers." Victoria gave her a seven. "Okay, after I check your vitals, we are going to give you some pain medicine, then we're going to see about taking out that tube. Sounds good?" Victoria nodded her head yes.

Raymond stroked her hair and kissed her forehead after the nurse left. "I can't wait for you to see our babies," he said. Again, Victoria looked puzzled. "Why are you looking like that?" asked Raymond. "She looked at me the same way when I told her you went to check on the babies," Nigel said. "You remember you had babies, right?" Raymond asked. Victoria nodded her head no, then put up one finger. Then Raymond said, "No, we had twins, a girl and a boy. They are beautiful." Victoria smiled and a tear fell from her eye. She hasn't had a chance to hold her son long at all and has never held her daughter.

Victoria tossed and turned in pain. She tried to sit up and move around, but nothing was working. She wondered where the nurse was with her medication. Nigel worried. He'd never seen Victoria in so much pain and made it his business to find that nurse.

A few moments later, the nurse and the doctor came into the room. The doctor checked her out told her how she was a miracle and how she had everyone worried about her. Then he gave her some pain medication, and she was soon off to sleep again. She looked good, according to the doctor, so he put in the orders to send her to the maternity ward by the end of the day.

Once she woke up and was released to the maternity ward, the doctor came into her room and spoke with both of them. Victoria looked even more worried. She sat up in the bed, and Raymond asked, "Is everything alright, doc?"

"It's never an easy thing to tell anyone…," the doctor said.

"Are the babies okay," Raymond asked?

"The babies are fine, but as you know, there were complications during the delivery. I believe, in my educated opinion, you should take precautions to prevent having any more babies. Victoria, your body, just can't handle it."

"You don't have to worry about it. I just found out I had twins, so I'm sure we're good…right, Ray?" Victoria said.

"You know it, baby," Raymond said.

"That's good to hear, but I would strongly consider making provisions so you don't," said the doctor.

"What do you suggest?" Raymond asked.

"A hysterectomy or Raymond getting a vasectomy," the doctor said.

"Tying my tubes won't help?" Victoria asked.

"Yes, it will. But it just wouldn't be best in your case because if you become pregnant again, it would be an ectopic pregnancy, and for you, that could be fatal," said the doctor.

"Is there more going on that you're not telling us?" Raymond asked.

"Nothing that you don't already know. I just wouldn't take any more chances," the doctor said.

"We will talk it over," Victoria said.

"I will check on you tomorrow. Have a good night and enjoy your babies," the doctor said.

"Yes, sir. Thank you," said Victoria.

After the doctor left, Victoria and Raymond talked it over. It take long to figure out what they were going to do. The vasectomy was going to happen. Neither one of them was concerned with having more children. They got their wish and answered prayer, plus a bonus. They agreed her health was their main priority, but there was one more pressing issue they hadn't discussed.

"Raymond, have you thought about a name for our daughter?"

"Yes."

"Well…what is it?"

"I held her in my arms and stared into her eyes, and the name that pressed upon my heart was Raychel, with a "y.""

"Sounds beautiful."

"You have to see her. She's beautiful."

"Seems like she already has you wrapped around her finger."

"Yes, she does, and Michael is definitely a momma's boy."

"Can you have the nurse bring the babies? I'm so ready to see them. I didn't get to hold them or anything."

"I'll be right back."

Raymond headed out of the nurse's station to give them the request. They brought the babies to the room, and Victoria's eyes filled with tears. She beheld her blessings and said to Raymond, "This love was worth waiting for." Nigel walked into the room, and Victoria said to him, "Come and hold your brother and sister." Then Raymond said, "Hold up. Let me get a picture with my family." Nigel stood afar off, not believing his father was talking to him. While Raymond got the camera on his phone ready, both he and Victoria said, "Come on, Nigel." Then Raymond said, "What you standing over there for? Get in the picture. Hold your sister." Nigel didn't want to smile too big, but he was happy about being included. They asked one of the nurses to take a picture with all of them in it. It was the family photo of a lifetime. Raymond uploaded it to his social media, tagging family and friends.

Later that week, the happy couple got to take home their babies. They loved them and made sure to make Nigel a part of it. Everyone came over to see them. Their pastor prayed over them and Raymond for the surgery he will need.

The Answer to Your Why

Over the years, Leigha and Joshua brought Ja'Miya over to play with Michael and Raychel. They grew up always playing with each other. They'd fight and go through what babies go through at that age. Their birthdays were only a few weeks apart, and it was like a royal celebration when their birthdays rolled around.

Joshua and Leigha had something important to discuss with Raymond and Victoria at the twin's fifth birthday party. They had no idea how to break the news to them. When the birthday party was over, they sat down on the couch in the living room while the twins and Ja'Miya played in the rec room. Raymond noticed they seemed to be on edge. He asked, "What's going on with y'all?

"What you mean?" Joshua asked.

"Man, we've been boys too long for this. What y'all on pins and needles for?" Raymond asked.

Leigha and Joshua looked at each other and with hesitation, sighed. Joshua said, "We got something to tell y'all."

"Is it that bad?" Victoria asked.

"You know we've been dealing with my mom being sick. She's gotten really bad. We have to move in with her to help her out," Leigha said.

"I know y'all didn't think you couldn't tell us that?" Raymond said.

"Yeah, you know we knew what you were going through with your mother, and whatever you need us to do, we'll do it. We are there for you guys." Victoria said.

"We are family, and y'all should know we got your back. You don't have to go through this alone," Raymond said.

"We know, but it was just as hard on us as it is on you. Our kids play together, we hang out all the time…y'all are family," Joshua said.

"What do you need from us?" Raymond asked.

"Just your support," Leigha said.

"Do you need any money, help moving, anything?" Raymond asked. Victoria sat quietly as their conversation continued. Leigha could feel the sadness. They had been besties for over 40 years and have never been apart.

"Just love and support?" Leigha said as tears fell down her face.

"Done!" Victoria said hugging her bestie.

"Look at me crying like some punk. Man, Jesus done made me soft. I have to choose between my mom and my best friend, who is like a sister to me. I don't want to go, but I don't want to stay. I want our kids to grow up together, but now they don't get to. Who will I talk to and clown with on the daily? Who will share a birthday party with Ja'Miya now? Who's going to be my strength when things get tough with my mom? I need to man up cause I don't do all this," Leigha said wiping the tears from her eyes. They all laughed.

Victoria melted. She responded to Leigha by saying, "I will be there for you any time you need me. I'm sorry. I know how hard this must have been for you. I'm really going to miss you, my friend." The ladies cried and hugged each other. Then Joshua said, "Look at these two saps. Just cryin' for no reason," and the men laughed and gave each other dap and a hug. Both wanted to cry, but they just mocked the ladies so that held it in.

A month later, Joshua and his family were off to his mother-in-law's house, saying goodbye to the only place they called home. They hoped to come back one day.

After their friends moved, Raymond and Victoria raised their twins and stayed in close contact with them throughout the years. It wasn't the same as hanging out with them though. They did visit Joshua and Leigha on milestone birthdays. They even vacationed together from time to time. Victoria and Raymond had their hands full, raising the twins and getting Nigel through school. Still, he graduated on time and with a B average. At the same time, Joshua and Leigha cared for her sick mother and welcomed their newest edition, a baby girl named LaLeia. They couldn't talk every day, but they understood no love was lost.

Raymond and Victoria were getting older in age, and the twins, Michael and Raychel, were enjoying high school. Time has flown by, and Victoria can't believe that they will be graduating high school in another year. Raymond groomed Michael in the family business of productions. Victoria tried to groom Raychel in interior decorating, but she'd rather get into acting and singing with her daddy. She wanted to support her children in their endeavors, no matter how much she wanted her daughter to follow in her footsteps. Raychel and Nigel were close. He created music for her, and they worked together all the time on music. He worked with his dad on the musical side of the business. He received his bachelor's in music and productions. He would teach his sister what he learned in college. It seemed as if all the children took after their father. This made Victoria a little sad. Nevertheless, she knew it was more important for the children to follow their destiny rather than what she wanted.

School has let out, and the twins are ready for the summer! Junior year is out the window, and senior year is vastly approaching. They have to get senior pictures done, deck out their new wardrobe, and get ready for the college of their choice. Raychel is ecstatic because she and her big brother have gigs set up at a few places. Nigel has been working hard to get them out there. Raymond helps them on the back end, but they don't want him to because they want to make it on their own. Michael has a secret he hasn't told anyone about. Raymond receives a surprise visit. Victoria longs for a protégé. Nigel still hasn't seen or heard from his mother, and by this time, he really doesn't care. I have plans for Michael, which is why I waited so long for Raymond and Victoria to birth him.

Their story is just beginning, but yours don't have to be. You can bring any turmoil in your marriage to an end. They had more than one A Love Worth Waiting For moment. Raymond and Victoria waited for their son a long time. They knew about him but didn't know about their daughter. Yet, I blessed their quiver because they went through so much. Raychel is called to an assignment as well. But my focus is Michael because he is chosen. Victoria waited for the love of her sister and is still in waiting. Raymond and Victoria longed for the love of Nigel. The love they also waited for was for each other. They had to learn to love one another before Michael's arrival. The love between a couple shouldn't diminish because of a troubled child, the loss of one, or of the one who has yet to arrive. You still love each other through it all. You look to fault each other, but the fault doesn't lie with either one of you. It is all about how to handle life and what it throws at you. The best way to win at that punch thrown at you is to battle it together. The enemy's trick is to make you see each other as an enemy. Don't fall for it. You don't have to lose at love, just be patient and wait on Me and trust I will send you the love you've been waiting for or restore the love that was lost and that you've been waiting to return.

A Love Worth Waiting For and My timing is everything to Raymond and his family. Is there still time to save this family? Do they even realize they need saving? What is this secret? Does it save, or will it destroy? Only time will tell.

The next book is: A Love Worth Waiting For: The Timing of God

Prayers

Prayer for Marriages

Father, in the name of Jesus, I lift up marriages before You. We need your help! You ordained marriage. It's one of the foundations of Your very being. You created it. You are the one who saw Adam in the garden by himself doing the day's work and saw it wasn't good for him to be alone. Then you fashioned the woman from his rib and called her to be a wife to him. They were called to each other, as are the husbands and wives today. We want to repent for leaving you out of the marriage, not seeking you concerning our marriages, not praying for our spouses, and neglecting who You've given us to love. Today, we welcome You into our marriages, into our hearts, to show us how to love and minister to one another without condition and without holding back love because of past hurts. Show us how to honor, respect, and submit one to another without feeling like we are losing ourselves in the process of being weak and vulnerable. We hold our spouse's heart in our hands, help us to take care of their heart as if it was our own. When we came together, You made us one flesh, not two. So, help us merge our lives synonymously, in harmony, and create beautiful in-tuned music together. Help us not to hold each other in bondage and in prison by using the forced keys of unforgiveness and bitterness. Cause our love to flow freely between one another by staying open with one another without offense. Be the glue in our marriages and get the glory that others may declare Your goodness, power, Your majesty, and love, in Jesus name I ask and pray. Amen.

Praying about God's Timing

Abba, Teacher, Creator of time, we beseech you now, coming boldly before your throne. We don't come lightly but respectful in all manner of conversation as we pray. We live in a time where everything is right now and quick. We don't even believe a prophecy because it doesn't come quickly. We become impatient waiting on that Word You gave us through your man or woman of God. Father, please forgive us for being impatient and moving as the world moves. Forgive us for doubting You and your word because it has yet to come to pass. Help us, teach us how to prepare for the promise instead of being impatient on the promise. Help us focus on You and growing with You while we patiently wait on the promise. Teach us about Your timing. Help us to understand it. Don't leave us blind. You said if we lack wisdom, to ask You for it, and You will freely give it to us. We're asking for Your wisdom right now, Abba. Be a teacher to us during this time. We will keep our ears open and sensitive to Your voice so we will know how to move and understand the purpose of the promise; that way, we know how to take care of the promise when it gets here; in Jesus' name, I ask and pray, Amen.

Prayer for Forgiveness

LORD, our Savior, Jesus the Christ, forgiver of all men regardless of what we've done, we pray for a heart that continuously forgives. We can't do it without You. It's hard, but we know it was even harder for You to send your Son to die for us, but you did it anyway, and we are thankful. You forgive us every single time we ask for it, and yet we won't extend that same forgiveness to our neighbor. Please forgive us. You said if we don't forgive those who hurt us, you won't forgive us. We don't want nor wish to be in the hands of an angry God. When we don't forgive our neighbor, that means You can't forgive us, which also means each sin we commit daily and sometimes eight or nine times a day, it is ever before You. When that happens, You can't do anything else but become angry because You see we haven't gotten it yet. Oh, how not to be in the hands of an angry God because we won't forgive. LORD, thy God, replace our heart of stone with a heart of flesh and cause us to truly become Your people and You our God. The very character of who You are is love, perfect love, which is why You can cast out all fear and anything that comes your way. Help us to understand we cause our own torment when we move in unforgiveness. LORD, our hearts hurt though and have been greatly damaged. You said You are near to those who have a broken heart and save those of a contrite spirit. We need saving, and we need you close. You want us to forgive at Your level, then show us how to do it and be there with us every step of the way. We don't want to hurt Your heart like ours have been hurt. We want our love to flow as freely as Yours does. Show us how the power of love can trump unforgiveness that we may walk in the fullness of Your image and character, in Jesus' name, I ask and pray. Amen.

ENCOURAGING SCRIPTURE PAGE

Mark 10:27 KJV
And Jesus looking upon them saith, With men it is impossible, but not
with God: for with God all things are possible.

Mark 11:24 KJV
Therefore I say unto you, What things soever ye desire, when ye pray,
believe that ye receive them, and ye shall have them.

Matthew 6:33 KJV
But seek ye first the kingdom of God, and his righteousness; and all
these things shall be added unto you.

Matthew 6:26 NIV
Look at the birds of the air; they do not sow or reap or store away in
barns, and yet your heavenly Father feeds them. Are you not much
more valuable than they?

Mark 9:23 NIV
"If you can'?" said Jesus. "Everything is possible for one who believes."

Isa 26:3 NKJV
You will keep him in perfect peace, Whose mind is stayed on You, Because he trusts in You.

Psalm 112:7 ESV
He is not afraid of bad news; his heart is firm, trusting in the LORD.

Hebrews 11:11-12 NIV

By faith Sarah herself received power to conceive, even when she was past the age, since she considered him faithful who had promised.

Therefore from one man, and him as good as dead, were born descendants as many as the stars of heaven and as many as the innumerable grains of sand by the seashore.

Gen 25:21 NIV

Isaac prayed to the LORD on behalf of his wife, because she was childless. The LORD answered his prayer, and his wife Rebekah became pregnant.

Psalm 113:9 NIV

He settles the childless woman in her home as a happy mother of children. Praise the LORD.

Luke 1:13 KJV

But the angel said unto him, Fear not, Zacharias: for thy prayer is heard; and thy wife Elisabeth shall bear thee a son, and thou shalt call his name John.

Phil 4:6-7 KJV

Be careful for nothing; but in every thing by prayer and supplication with thanksgiving let your requests be made known unto God.

And the peace of God, which passeth all understanding, shall keep your hearts and minds through Christ Jesus.

Psalm 130:5 KJV

I wait for the LORD, my soul doth wait, and in his word do I hope.

Gen 1:22 KJV
And God blessed them, saying, Be fruitful, and multiply, and fill the waters in the seas, and let fowl multiply in the earth.

I Sam 2:21 NLT
And the LORD gave Hannah three sons and two daughters. Meanwhile, Samuel grew up in the presence of the LORD.

Gen 30:22
And God remembered Rachel, and God hearkened to her, and opened her womb.

Luke 1:36-37 NLT
What's more, your relative Elizabeth has become pregnant in her old age! People used to say she was barren, but she has conceived a son and is now in her sixth month.
For nothing is impossible with God.

Rom 12:12
Rejoicing in hope; patient in tribulation; continuing instant in prayer;

Psalm 27:14
Wait on the LORD;
Be of good courage,
And He shall strengthen your heart;
Wait, I say, on the LORD!

Isa 40:30-31
Even the youths shall faint and be weary,
And the young men shall utterly fall,
But those who wait on the LORD

Shall renew their strength;
They shall mount up with wings like eagles,
They shall run and not be weary,
They shall walk and not faint.

Deu 7:14 NLT

You will be blessed above all the nations of the earth. None of your men or women will be childless, and all your livestock will bear young.

Ex 23:25-26 NLT

"You must serve only the LORD your God. If you do, I will bless you with food and water, and I will protect you from illness.
There will be no miscarriages or infertility in your land, and I will give you long, full lives.

Isa 66:9 NIV

Do I bring to the moment of birth and not give delivery?" says the LORD. "Do I close up the womb when I bring to delivery?" says your God.

Gen 1:28 NIV

God blessed them and said to them, "Be fruitful and increase in number; fill the earth and subdue it. Rule over the fish in the sea and the birds in the sky and over every living creature that moves on the ground."

Rom 4:17-18 NIV

As it is written: "I have made you a father of many nations." He is our father in the sight of God, in whom he believed—the God who gives life to the dead and calls into being things that were not.
Against all hope, Abraham in hope believed and so became the father of many nations, just as it had been said to him, "So shall your offspring be."

About the Author

Keisha Lapsley
keycitypro@gmail.com
www.authorklap.com

<u>Books</u>
Homeless: My Favorite Park Bench
Homeless 2: Stained Worship (Coming Soon)
Who Said Love Doesn't Hurt?
Jesus the Janitor
The Gift of Helps: Learning When to Say NO!
No Mo' Explainin'!
I Did It Wrong!
Gem of a Lady
My Writing Belongs to Him (male/female version)

<u>Mentor Writing Courses</u>
Self-pace Webinar
Keys to Writing 6-week Online Course
Keys to Writing VIP Upgrade Online Course

KeyCity Enterprise is looking for actors for upcoming web series and television shows.
Please submit all resumes & links to reels to keycitypro@gmail.com
Book Cover Photos Credits: Pexels: Johnathan Borba, Emmanuel Ajayi, Dellon Thomas & Pixabay: Haider Tahir, Ariprodz,

www.ingramcontent.com/pod-product-compliance
Lightning Source LLC
Chambersburg PA
CBHW051221210726
48290CB00003B/742